He kissed her.

It was like the igniting of torches. The world spun deliciously. Tilted. Then righted itself.

They stood for some time looking out toward the bay. A sprinkling of stars was shining in the dark sky and just a tiny sliver of a moon made a silver arc above them. Michael kept one arm securely around Susan and held her tightly to him.

At last the pounding of her heart subsided to below the level of the beating waves. "Let's walk a bit," she said and pulled slightly ahead of him to move down the beach. Each lost in thought, they walked wordlessly for some time with Susan in the lead.

Suddenly she gave a small cry. "Oh, that's cold!" Intending to walk parallel to the water, she had mindlessly walked into the foamy tide.

"You know, I really worry about you," Michael said, drawing her back up on the dry sand. "Don't you ever watch where you're going?"

He was always so calm—so self-possessed. "Don't *you* ever get rattled? Doesn't anything *ever* overwhelm you?"

He was quiet for a moment. Even in the dim light she could see his gray eyes looking at her. "It's called living by faith." The words were spoken as softly as a prayer.

She recoiled as if he'd slapped her. In the joy of his company, in the rapture of his embrace, she had forgotten the gulf that separated them. The phrase was trite but they really did live in two different worlds.

"I want to go in now," she said sadly.

LOVE UNMERITED

Donna Fletcher Crow

Serenade/Serenata
BOOKS
of the Zondervan Publishing House
Grand Rapids, Michigan

A Note From the Author:
I love to hear from my readers! You may correspond with me b
writing:

    Donna F. Crow
    1415 Lake Drive S.E.
    Grand Rapids, MI 49506

LOVE UNMERITED
Copyright © 1986 by Donna F. Crow
    3-00
Serenade/Serenata is an imprint of Zondervan
Publishing House, 1415 Lake Drive, S.E.,
Grand Rapids, Michigan 49506.

ISBN 0-310-47442-6

All Scripture quotations, unless otherwise noted, are taken from the
King James Version of the Bible.

Edited by Ann McMath
Designed by Kim Koning

Printed in the United States of America

86 87 88 89 90 91 / 10 9 8 7 6 5 4 3 2 1

Mahalo
To
Debbie and Jan

*Where the Spirit of the Lord is,
there is freedom.*

2 Corinthians 3:17b

CHAPTER 1

SUSAN JAMISON SAT at her desk, frowning at the hopeless muddle in front of her. She was considered the best public relations person the Langford Hotel in San Francisco had ever had, so when the PR girl in their newly opened resort in Kauai walked off the job giving barely three-hour's notice, Susan agreed to go pick up the pieces. Now she was wondering if the wreck was salvageable.

"Miss Jamison?" The deep voice jarred her reverie.

Susan turned to the figure before her, her eyes first focusing on tailored blue slacks and a blue sport shirt opened at the neck to reveal a golden tan, then moving slowly, up the angular planes of a forceful jawline and cheekbones to stop abruptly at spirited gray eyes.

She almost gasped. "I thought gray eyes existed only in novels," she murmured. Then she blushed a hot pink. What a very unprofessional thing to say.

But the gray eyes didn't seem to mind. They

twinkled at her appreciatively. "I'm Michael Travis." After a moment's pause, he added, "About the convention arrangements."

She stole a sideways glance at her appointment calendar. This morning, March 11, was blank. The afternoon was jammed to overflowing, but this morning appeared blessedly free. It was imperative that the morning be free if Susan were to have any hope of dealing with the chaos her predecessor left behind. She regained her composure quickly. "I'm sorry, you don't seem to have an appointment." He showed no signs of moving. "But I suppose I can work you in," she said with a barely suppressed sigh.

"That's very good of you." He grinned, and seated himself in the chair in front of her desk.

Susan felt herself blushing again, this time at his unsettling smile. *Unprofessional*, she scolded herself, and hoped the rebuke would help her get her mind back on business. If there was anything she despised in her demanding occupation, it was unprofessionalism.

"Now, what can I do for you, Mr.—ah—Travis, was it?"

"Yes, I've come to talk to you about the arrangements for our convention in May. I believe you have my letter."

Susan opened the file drawer in her desk. She could only hope his letter had been filed properly before her arrival. Surprisingly enough, it was there. "Oh, yes. Travis. Here it is," she said with some relief, pulling a long manila file folder from the drawer. "Now let's see . . ." As she spoke, her eyes scanned the letter in front of her. "You want to make arrangements for a convention in mid-May for the Christian Lawyers Association . . ." She stopped in midsentence.

She didn't like lawyers. Of all the professions in the world she had the least respect for lawyers—a pack

8

of shysters, all of them. She thought fleetingly, but bitterly of the small inheritance a crooked lawyer had cheated her out of. . . .

And she didn't like Christians. Again, her thoughts were rapid and bitter as she remembered the long-faced hypocrites who had populated the campus of the small Bible college she had been sent to by her uncle. It hadn't taken her long to decide that if that was Christianity she didn't need it.

"Miss Jamison, is anything wrong?"

"Oh, no, not at all." She collected her scattered thoughts. *Professionalism* she reminded herself sternly. "It says here that you expect about one hundred fifty lawyers, most of whom will be bringing their spouses." As she spoke the word her eyes involuntarily sought his left hand.

He caught her look and smiled, holding up a ringless hand. "That's right, those who have spouses, that is. We should have about two hundred fifty to three hundred in attendance. I understood that this hotel could handle that number."

"Yes, certainly. Since your convention date is almost two months away, as long as we know precisely what your plans are and what you expect from us there should be no problem at all. We pride ourselves on smoothly run conventions. Not many hotels on Kauai provide convention facilities."

"Yes, I know. That's why we chose the Langford. And as to specific arrangements, that's what I'm here for." He was studying her in the most disconcerting manner. Every time she looked up into those perceptive gray eyes she felt her heart lurch.

"You're president of the organization?" It said so on the letter she was holding right in front of her, but she had to say something to cover her confusion.

"Yes. Heather, our executive secretary at CLA headquarters normally handles these details, but I was

9

due a vacation, and since I hadn't been to Kauai for more years than I like to think about, I grabbed it as a convenient excuse."

Opportunist, she thought. Just what she'd expect from a lawyer—probably charging it all to some client, too.

"So, you've been here before?"

"Yes, my parents used to vacation here regularly when I was a child." He paused. "I loved the island, but haven't been back since Dad died when I was in high school. I hope I won't find it too changed."

"I wouldn't know about that. I've been here less than twenty-four hours myself. Now why don't you outline what you have in mind for your daily program and we'll start by allotting the meeting rooms you'll need. Then we can talk about schedules, entertainment, and optional sightseeing tours."

At her desk in San Francisco Susan could have immediately laid her hands on the precise forms she needed to record these plans, as well as known the dimensions and seating capacity of each meeting room in the hotel by heart. But now, she realized with a sense of panic that she hadn't even seen any of the meeting rooms at the Langford Kauai. The General Manager had given her a floor plan and map when she arrived yesterday afternoon and advised her to "get acquainted with the premises." She wasn't even acquainted with her desk yet.

She made notes as Michael Travis outlined the proposed schedule for the three-day seminar: "Meetings, workshops, and panel discussions every morning from nine o'clock until noon with a coffee break in between, afternoons free for relaxation and sightseeing. Most mornings we'll need at least three rooms as we offer a choice of seminars."

"Will you want all meals provided by the hotel?"

"Only breakfast and dinner, I think," he replied after brief consideration.

"A wise choice," she nodded and made notes on her paper. "People like to be free to explore on their own some, and if they've paid for all their meals with their room they'll feel tied to their hotel. Now I suggest we take a look at the meeting rooms so you can select the ones best suited to your needs." Susan took a ring of keys from the top drawer of her desk and led the way across the small office. The skirt of her colorfully striped dress swished with her long legs. When she reached the door she turned back and caught the gray eyes looking at her slim ankles. He smiled, unembarrassed, and followed her out the door.

The Langford Kauai, as with most island hotels, was built in a tropical style only partially enclosed so that even in early March the fresh breezes swept through the lobby and corridors. In the center of the lobby she paused by a two-story mosaic terrace with a waterfall cascading over it. Above, the ceiling was open to the sky and the plants around the fish pond grew luxuriantly in the natural sunlight, fresh air, and rainfall they received. Michael Travis observed the colorful sunfish swimming in the pool beneath the waterfall while his guide got her bearings.

Susan glanced quickly at the hotel floorplan she held. "Right down this corridor, Mr. Travis," she said in her most professional tones, trying to cover the fact that she wasn't sure where she was going.

"Since we'll be working together for some time on this, why don't you call me Michael," he suggested.

"All right—Michael. And our guests usually call me Susan," she managed a smile. "Ah, here we are." She stopped so abruptly he almost ran into her, and his hand went to her waist to avert a collision. After he removed it, she still felt the warmth of his firm clasp. Ordering herself to ignore it, she inserted the master key in the locked door.

She gasped as her hand flicked on the lightswitch just inside the door.

"I think this will be a little small for our purposes." Michael's voice was lively with amusement.

They were standing in a service closet.

Susan backed out and shut the door hastily. "Wrong door, obviously," she said stiffly. "I'm sorry." What a fool she felt. What he must be thinking of her. She looked again at her map of the hotel. That should have been the right door.

"It must be this one," she tried to speak brightly as she fussed with the key.

The door opened on a well-stocked linen room. *If he laughs at me I'll just tell him where he can take his convention of fraudulent fanatics.*

"Perhaps you would allow me?" He took the floorplan from her hand. Susan shot him a defiant look, but he wasn't laughing. Smiling—but not laughing.

"It looks like we took the wrong corridor from the lobby. Shall we try again?"

Susan nodded and turned sharply toward the lobby. She was seething inside. Not only did she not know this hotel, apparently she didn't even know how to read a simple floorplan. She had never looked so incompetent in her life. And none of it was her fault. Why did he have to show up on her first morning when she'd been in her office for less than twenty minutes? What right did he have to come here and demand her services without an appointment and then laugh at her with those smirking gray eyes?

She held her shoulders stiff beneath the blue linen jacket that topped her dress. Her little upturned nose went a fraction higher in the air, and she gave a defiant shake of her long, honey-colored hair as she preceded him back to the lobby.

Susan was concentrating so hard on her dignity that

12

she stepped right in front of an autocratic-looking elderly lady who was being solicitously accompanied to the front desk by a young man in a chauffeur's livery. Susan muttered an apology and turned down the corridor to her left.

"Now, this looks more promising," Michael said, pausing before a door marked *Halawai* and holding out his hand for the keys.

Susan ignored his outstretched hand and opened the room herself. Did he think she couldn't even turn a key?

"Yes, this looks fine. Appropriately named, too," he commented, surveying the room.

She looked at him blankly. "Named?"

"Yes, the name on the door translates 'meeting.'"

They quickly surveyed the other conference rooms, Susan jotting notes on her clipboard of the uses Michael felt his group could make of the various facilities.

"How about continuing this over lunch?" Michael suggested, glancing at his watch.

"My goodness, I had no idea it was lunch time already!" She couldn't believe that the morning could really be gone. And all the work she had planned was still undone. "I'm sorry, but I won't have time for lunch. My afternoon is scheduled full."

"Then how about dinner?"

"I'm sorry, Mr. Travis . . ."

"Michael."

"Michael," she said resignedly. "I'm afraid tomorrow afternoon is the soonest I can get back to your convention. But you did say you were staying for several days, didn't you?"

"Tomorrow afternoon then. How about a late lunch poolside?"

"Yes, that will be fine. One o'clock." She turned and walked quickly away, her high-heeled sandals

13

clicking on the smooth marble hallway. She would have agreed to anything just to get away. This morning had been definitely too much!

And if her morning was too much, her afternoon was even worse: Three jet-set guests were to be plied with cocktails at the poolside bar, then posed by the house photographer for the hotel's publicity sheet, "Aloha"; details were to be finalized for the Langford's Japanese barbecue at which descendants of Hawaiian royalty were to be present for the annual Prince Kuhio Days celebration; and the filming of a television commercial to be shown in six major cities on the mainland had to be supervised.

It wasn't until late that evening when Susan was finally back in her hotel room relaxing in a short cotton robe after a quick refreshing shower, that her mind returned to the events of the morning. She took a sip of the white wine she had asked room service to bring with her small fruit salad and chicken sandwich. As she sat back in her chair and looked out at the rolling blue Pacific beyond her lanai, she saw again those remarkable gray eyes. In the books gray eyes were always cold and hard—glinting like steel. But these were different, much different; she had never seen such kind eyes with such appealing crinkles of humor at the corners.

And yet she sensed a reserve of strength radiating from the man even as he stood before her in her imagination. She had no doubt that those eyes could become hard and cold. She shivered involuntarily; she would not like to be the target of those shafts of steel and ice if they should have reason to spark.

Well, he can just take his sexy gray eyes and flash them elsewhere. She bit fiercely into her sandwich. *Between the two of them, God and lawyers have managed to take everything I ever had—and that was little enough to start with. And Mr. high-and-mighty smirking Travis stands for both!*

The next morning, dressed in a softly gathered, bright red skirt and a crisp white blouse piped in red, Susan was actually able to spend some uninterrupted time making sense of the disorder on her desk. From what she saw there, she could tell that the girl who walked off the job so precipitously had actually done the Langford Kauai a favor. How she'd ever managed to get hired in the first place was a mystery. Susan paused to wonder how her former assistant who had temporarily stepped into Susan's old job in San Francisco was faring. Linda was a conscientious worker and had spent six months working under Susan's direction, so she should be equipped to handle the promotion.

A shrill ringing from the phone on her desk interrupted Susan's thoughts. The familiar masculine voice at the other end of the line brought a smile to her lips. "Josh, you must be telepathic—I was just thinking about home."

"Glad to hear you still consider San Francisco home. Does that mean you'll be coming back soon?"

"I don't know Josh. Things are in a mess here. They really needed me, and I certainly can't leave until everything is under control."

"So where does that leave us? Susie, you know how I felt about your accepting that job. Surely someone else—"

"Josh, we've been over that ground a thousand times, and I don't want to hash it out again long distance. It's so good to hear your voice, surely you didn't call just to pick a fight?"

"I called in hopes of hearing that you were interviewing for someone to take the job there and you'd have some idea of when you'd be back. I don't like having 2,500 miles of ocean between me and my girl."

Susan sighed, "I know, Josh. Thanks for calling.

15

I'll send you a progress report as soon as I've made some progress to report on."

"And in the meantime I can just sit on it, right? Talk to ya later, Baby." And he hung up.

Susan sat for several seconds letting the receiver dangle loosely across her thumb before she hung up with a shake of her head. Josh just couldn't understand her commitment to her job. He viewed it as simply something to pass the time until she settled down and married him. And why it was taking her so long to be about it was beyond him.

A flash of the digital clock on her desk caught her eye. One o'clock already! She hated herself for having agreed to meet Mr. Travis—no, Michael—for lunch, but business was business. The customer was almost never right, but he had to be allowed to think he was. Susan refreshed her mocha almond lipstick, enhanced the bounce in her golden hair with a few flicks of her hairbrush and made her way to the poolside restaurant.

As she crossed the grounds, Susan noted with appreciation the Langford Kauai's scheme of water decoration. It was an engineering and landscaping feat that was one of their prime attractions. She had read that it had already caught the attention of several design magazines for its ecological soundness as well as its beauty. But this was her first chance to view for herself the ponds and streams that so cleverly enhanced the landscape and delighted all that came near it: fish and waterfowl who made it their habitat; tourists who never tired of strolling in the luxuriant gardens and across the little footbridge; and the jungle vegetation that grew in verdant banks and never languished, even in the dry season. The water was then filtered and circulated into an elaborate pool system designed so that the swimmer could float from one palm-surrounded pool to another, beneath an arched footbridge, and then in final triumph, under a waterfall.

Susan finally arrived at the poolside restaurant tucked behind the waterfall. She was delighted with this spot where diners could eat accompanied by the gentle sounds of falling water while looking through the curtain of silver droplets, across the aquamarine pool, past the well-groomed strip of white sand beach, out to the rolling surf beyond.

Michael rose as she walked toward him. She tried not to let herself be impressed by his crisp white slacks and white linen Philippine sport shirt. But she couldn't help noticing the open neckline that revealed a hint of bronze hair on his chest.

He guided her to a table seemingly right under the waterfall, although there was no fear of getting wet. As she listened to the gentle strumming of steel guitars and the soothing splashes of the falling crystal water, and watched the snorkelers bobbing with the waves in the bay and surfers catching the big waves farther out, she suddenly felt the tension of the morning dissolve. The irritation aroused by Josh's phone call seemed ages away. It was as if no unpleasantness could possibly penetrate into this hideaway.

Other than a friendly greeting when she arrived, Michael had hardly spoken a word. She looked across the table at him now, a curl of his dark blond hair falling on his forehead as he studied the menu. "What do you recommend?" he asked.

"Don't ask me," Susan laughed. "So far I've had two chicken sandwiches and an order of scrambled eggs on toast. You're the one who's practically a native."

"All right then, may I order for you?"

"Please do," she laid her unopened menu down. After Michael gave their order they became so entranced watching a pair of expert surfers that they didn't even notice when their luncheons were set in front of them.

"Look, he's waiting for the big wave. . . . Here it comes. . . . I hope he makes it this time," Michael narrated.

"Oh, it went clear over him," Susan cried.

"No, look, he rode through the tube, he's out at the other end," Michael's voice mirrored the surfer's triumph.

"What a thrill that must be—it's thrilling just to watch." Susan was almost breathless.

"Now look, the other one isn't riding the wave in to shore, he's turning over it and heading back to sea."

Susan held her breath, then said with genuine disappointment, "Oh, he didn't make it! That must be a terribly difficult thing to do." She leaned forward for a better view and almost put her arm in the salad. "Oh, where did that come from?" she laughed.

They continued to be entertained by the surfers as they ate papaya salads garnished with vanda orchids. Susan was fascinated by the lushness of this paradise. "They use orchids here like we do parsley at home."

When the salads had been removed and the waiter had served the tea Susan requested, she brought out her clipboard. "Now, we really ought to get down to business if we're going to get this convention planned in proper Langford tradition."

But with the mention of business returned the reality of Michael's business. She had been wrong— the secluded hideaway was not impenetrable by unpleasantness. And the unpleasantness was hers.

"Just what do your Christian lawyers *do* in your association? Hold prayer meetings?"

But Michael didn't appear nonplussed by her challenge. "Well, we do believe in prayer," he smiled. "But our purpose as a professional organization is to promote freedom of religion, help in freedom of expression cases that apply to religious issues, and assist lawyers who want to help their clients reconcile rather than litigate."

"You mean freedom of *your* religion, of course."

"Not at all." He shook his head with a slight smile. "The same court decision that would prevent a group of Jewish students from having a club meeting at school, for example, would also deny freedom of expression to evangelicals, or vice versa. Which group happens to be used as the test case is really immaterial."

Susan quickly saw that engaging in a verbal battle with a lawyer could have its drawbacks. She changed her tack. "But surely, if your clients reconcile rather than going to court, the attorney looses out on his fat fees." Now she had him.

He smiled slowly, the gray eyes twinkling. "But some of us are in this profession for something more important than our bank accounts."

"Yours must be a *very* small organization."

"Perhaps we could find a more palatable topic for conversation if we gave ourselves to menu planning," he suggested mildly.

"That is normally handled by catering," Susan said, but in her "the customer is always right" attitude she added, "but we can cover the broad outlines. Breakfasts we usually do buffet style. That allows the maximum range for individual tastes and is the quickest way to serve a group. If that's agreeable to you we can move right on to dinners."

Michael nodded.

"Very well. For your first night I would suggest our dishless dinner. It's very attractive, tasty, and unusual."

"Good, tell me about it."

"The tables are spread with banana leaves and

19

branches of bougainvillaea blossoms. First we serve papaya soup, in green papaya shells, followed by a seafood-topped lettuce salad with house dressing in abalone shells. Our special Hawaiian Pineapple Chicken is served individually in pineapple halves, accompanied by rice wrapped in ti leaves. Dessert is coconut sherbet in coconut halves."

"That sounds great!"

She was gratified by his enthusiastic endorsement. She had stayed awake half the night dreaming it up. She had to have something to show him that she knew her job. "Now, about wines—I'll arrange an appointment for you with our wine steward."

"That won't be necessary."

"Oh." No, of course it wouldn't—the evils of liquor had been one of the favorite harangues of speakers at college. "Do you require your members to take the pledge in order to save them from hellfire?" She hated the sarcastic note in her voice.

But rather than flaring back, he completely disconcerted her by laughing. "No, nothing like that. But lawyers of all people, have cause to see the results of overindulgence—both in the lives of our clients and our colleagues. So we don't promote it in the organization. Our members' personal lives are their own affair."

"My, my—aren't we broad-minded." Again, she hated herself. Everything she said came out wrong.

"Guess I was wrong about menu planning being a safe topic," Michael grinned at her. "Do you think we dare try sightseeing schedules?"

Susan put a clean sheet on top of her clipboard. "Yes, of course. What do you have in mind?"

"Well, one afternoon we could do the south shore: Spouting Horn, Wiamea Canyon, perhaps the botanical gardens. Another day the north shore: Kilauea Point, the caves, Lumahai Beach . . ." He broke off in midsentence and smiled at the blank look on her face.

Susan started to bristle at his show-off superiority, then realized there was no way she could hide the fact that in island matters she was a novice, so she smiled and joined his amusement. "You're speaking in a foreign language. I don't even know how to write those things down much less plan a tour to them."

"I forgot you're a *makaikai*," he said.

"A what? Watch what you say now. Don't get the idea you can get away with anything just because I don't speak the language yet."

"Don't worry, I just called you a newcomer. But seriously, getting to know the island is important to your job—and to my convention, incidentally. How about letting me show you the places that should be on your agenda?"

She hesitated; what he said made sense, but he had made no attempt to hide the fact that he found her attractive. Was this just an excuse to make a play for her? "I don't really think I'd have time. I need to get acquainted with my office before I begin exploring the island."

"Now how many hotel guests are going to ask for a tour of your office?"

"But you have no idea what shambles things are in. . . ." She stood her ground.

"If they're that bad, a few more days won't make a difference, will it? And think of how much more helpful you can be to all your guests as soon as you know what choices are available. Now, just supposing you wake up tomorrow and find it pouring rain. When you arrive at your office seventeen guests are waiting for you—drenched with rain and disappointed because their snorkeling expedition has been cancelled. What do you suggest as an alternative?"

She was silent. "Well, suppose you tell me, Mr. Chamber of Commerce?"

"I fully intend to. For those possessed of umbrellas and waterproof shoes the botanical gardens are still pleasant in the rain, a tour of the sugar cane plantation can be accompanied in a jeep, dry-eyed and dry-soled, or rumor has it the new shopping arcade is relatively undercover and a delight to tourists. Now see how a knowledge of the territory can aid your job, enhance your profession, and benefit your guests?" he finished with a flourish. "The defense rests."

Susan sat shaking her head. "You really are impossible, how can I argue against all that. I'll try to work you into my schedule."

"Fine. I'll meet you in the lobby at nine o'clock in the morning."

And all the rest of the day Susan was unaccountably happy. She didn't think of Josh's phone call once.

CHAPTER 2

EVEN THE GRAY CLOUDS in the sky couldn't dim Susan's excitement the next morning. As a matter of fact, she had suddenly become rather fond of the color gray. She found herself humming softly as she dressed in white slacks and a bright yellow blouse. The sense of anticipation, of course, was for the sightseeing, she told herself. Even Ted Rawlings, the General Manager of the Langford had endorsed the idea that she needed to be acquainted with the island in order to do her job well.

She was ready a full fifteen minutes early. But she couldn't go down early—it would never do to show such eagerness. She stepped out onto her lanai and stood for several minutes listening to the rustling of the palm trees and the crashing of the surf a few hundred feet beyond. The inescapable water sounds of the island were already becoming a part of her life.

Susan stepped back into her room, picked up her large straw bag and the jacket that matched her slacks and decided that if she walked very slowly she could

23

start now. She went out of her room, turned right, and had gone about twenty feet before she realized she was going the wrong way. A sense of direction had never been one of her gifts, but this was ridiculous! *What is the matter with me?* She turned and walked toward the elevators, glad there had been no one in the hall to see her.

Michael was waiting by the fish pond and rose to meet her when the elevator opened across the lobby. He was wearing trim white jeans and a silvery blue shirt that made her even more stunningly aware of his leonine hair and gray eyes.

"Shall we have breakfast here before we start?" he suggested.

They found seats on the terrace by the upper end of the pool system, but just under the sheltering roof. Susan sat in a big basket chair with its wicker back spread out like a fanned tail of a peacock. "We call this a princess chair," the waitress said, flashing a charming Polynesian smile. "It's where royalty would sit for a festivity. So I guess that means you're a princess today."

"Thank you," Susan was pleased and slightly embarrassed—after all, this was a business excursion.

"She's right, you know," Michael said when the waitress had gone.

Susan didn't want to meet his gaze, so she stared instead at the two small, red, heart-shaped anthurium in the white bud vase on the center of the table— Hawaii's valentine flower.

When Michael had been served his Ham Steak Hawaiian with glazed pineapple and bananas, and she her Omelet Foo Young, her guide produced a small map and began pointing out items of interest. "I had hoped to take you to the north shore today—the beauty there is incredible—but I'm afraid we'll have to save that for a sunnier day. Spring weather is unpredictable in the islands. Its best to be flexible. I think we should head to the south side to look for the sunshine." He traced a line on the map with his finger. "Can you be away the whole day?"

Susan nodded. "Ted—he's the General Manager, so that makes him everyone's boss at the hotel— thinks it's a great idea. Some press ladies are having a luncheon here today and he even offered to fill in for me. The ladies are sure to be happier with Ted anyway."

"Great. Let's go then."

They had just left the Terrace Room when a lovely young Hawaiian girl with thick black hair hanging well below her waist and a brilliant red hibiscus blossom at her temple hurried up.

"I'm sorry to interrupt, Miss Jamison, but Catering asked that you check the menu for the luncheon today before you leave." She handed Susan a sheaf of papers on a clipboard.

"Yes, of course, just a minute. Lani, this is Mr. Travis. We're planning a convention for his organization. Michael, Lani Akamu is Ted Rawling's secretary and my part-time assistant."

Lani and Michael talked briefly while Susan looked through the papers. "Yes, Lani, this looks fine. Tell the chef to make it the passion fruit sherbet rather than the coconut pie for dessert."

Lani smiled and departed gracefully, her long hair swaying behind her, the long skirt of her floral print dress falling softly against her legs.

"Yes, the island girls are lovely, aren't they?" Susan teased Michael whose gaze was following the retreating girl.

"I knew I'd been away too long," he said with a devilish grin and took Susan's elbow to usher her out of the hotel.

In the parking lot he seated her in a sporty little gunmetal blue car. When he turned the key in the ignition it chimed like a clock. "Oh, what a charming surprise," Susan laughed.

"Yes, much nicer than those irritating buzzers screaming at you to fasten your seat belt," Michael agreed as he leaned across to help Susan with her seatbelt. She savored his light Spice Islands after-shave and caught herself in a barely suppressed desire to touch his thick wavy locks before he leaned back into his seat. The emotion left her shaken. *I must be missing Josh more than I realized*, she thought.

They drove past miles of tall green sugar cane fields that seemingly ran right up to the base of green mountains in the distance. "See where all those clouds are congregating over there?" Michael pointed to his right, "That's Mount Wai'ale'ale, the wettest place on earth. About 500 inches of rain a year, I think. The mountain hides under the tradewind clouds every afternoon and the resulting rainfall overflows into Wiamean Canyon where we're going."

"I don't like all this talk of wet clouds. I thought I came here for sunshine." Susan made a face.

"All this lush tropical growth has to be watered. But the clouds disappear every night when the menehunes wake up and prepare the island land-scapes for the next day's viewing."

"Mene-what?"

"The local legendary little people, like leprechauns. They even built a giant fish pond that's still in use for raising mullet. The pond has a stone wall more than nine-hundred-feet long. It was constructed in a single night, the way the tiny people do everything." Michael was recounting the legend with a perfectly straight face, as if giving a history lesson.

"Do they have superpowers?" Susan asked, also in complete seriousness.

"No, there's just an awful lot of them and they work very hard."

"That sounds like a very convenient legend—now I'll know who to blame things on." They laughed together, and as Michael glanced at her with his dancing eyes Susan felt something like an electric shock go through her. She had known this man for less than two days; he stood for everything she despised—dishonesty, fanaticism, hypocrisy. How could she possibly be enjoying his company so much?

Michael handed her the map, "If you follow our progress, it'll help to orient you."

She obediently looked at the chart in front of her. "Queen Victoria's Profile? What's that?" she asked.

"Coming right up." Michael pulled to a stop by a metal roadsign bearing the insignia of a Hawaiian warrior in a flowing red and gold cape and feathered helmet.

They faced a mountain range to their left. "Do you see it?" Michael pointed to the green ridge.

"Well, maybe. Which way is she lying?" Susan frowned.

"Head to the south, see her sharp nose, rounded forehead, then the flowing little veil she always wore?"

"Well . . . someone sure had to work at that," Susan laughed. "Am I supposed to arrange a tour to this?"

"Hey, hold on—I'm working up to the big stuff."

They drove on and were soon inside a lacy green tunnel of eucalyptus trees. Their flowing branches arched over the highway like a great gothic cathedral. Suddenly they emerged at the end of the tunnel, and to Susan's delight, into sunlight.

"I was hoping that would happen," Michael replied to her joy at seeing the sun. "If there's to be sun anywhere on the island, it'll be here. And another piece of luck, it looks like we're just in time for a ceremony for Prince Kuhio Days." Michael stopped the car near another Hawaiian warrior sign that proclaimed this to be Prince Kuhio park. He helped Susan from the car and they strolled among the gaily colored mumu and flowered-shirt clad spectators and found a seat on the low stone wall. On the green hillside across a lagoon was a monument marking the Prince's birthplace. A row of dignitaries was seated in front of the monument, the ladies in long white dresses, the men in red and gold capes like those worn by ancient islanders. A ladies' choir concluded a song and then a speaker rose to tell of the service the prince had rendered to his people: Slated to rule the Kingdom of Hawaii, Prince Kuhio had been educated in England and groomed by Queen Liliuokalani to succeed her. But he found his throne swept from under him when the Queen was deposed. Instead of living in Europe as exiled royalty, the prince chose to serve his people as the first elected representative to Congress where, though having no vote, he used his persuasive powers to try to help Kanai.

Prince Kuhio and his wife, Princess Elizabeth, were represented at the festival by a stunning young island couple, he in a black tuxedo and ruffled shirt with a wide purple satin banner across his chest, she in an ivory satin Victorian-style dress with a flowing red banner that draped behind her into a sweeping train.

As Michael and Susan listened to the ceremonies, children frolicked at their feet and groups of islanders picnicked in the green park. Native girls in flowered dresses wearing wreaths of leaves on their heads and leis of purple flowers and green leaves, representing the colors of Kauai, passed among the spectators selling little bags of bright red snack food. Michael bought one and offered some to Susan.

She hesitated. "What is it?"

"Pickled mangoes. A local delicacy."

Susan sampled one gingerly. "Sour." She made a face. And again they were laughing together. Being so comfortable with Michael made her uncomfortable.

They left the festival in progress and drove on along the sparkling blue Pacific waters. Michael pulled into a parking lot bordered by intensely red geraniums and a stretch of green grass beyond.

As he held the door for Susan to step out onto the red asphalt surface, Michael warned, "Be careful of your slacks. This red clay is awful stuff. It'll stain anything it touches."

Susan endeavored to follow his advice and stepped carefully as he led her over a gentle rise. Suddenly she was confronted with a breathtaking view of surf crashing on a wide ledge of black lava. As the oncoming waves thundered in, a great white saltwater geyser spewed spectacularly from a hole in the rocks.

"Oh," Susan cried involuntarily as a mist of salt water fell on her.

They stood for some time listening to the roaring, whooshing sound of water under the lava and watching in fascination each display of the Spouting Horn, followed by a moment of calm as the wet drops fell back into the water pooled on the lava ledge and dissolved in white foam.

"Listen," Michael said quietly after a few minutes. "It's a sleeping dragon. He's curled up under the lava and whenever a wave comes in he snorts the water out. You can hear his breathing."

Just then some tourists returned from a walk on the lava ledge and told a couple nearby, "You really should go down—there's a trail all the way. It starts just past the sign that says 'Enter at Your Own Risk.'"

Susan and Michael could hardly contain their laughter until the tourists had gone. "Come on," he said, taking her hand. "That sounds too inviting to miss."

He led her under the boughs of lacy pines with their tiny cones and long tufted needles swaying in the sea air. The promised trail was red clay.

"I think we'd better do something about protecting these white pants," he said, and stooped down to roll up the legs of both their pants. As he did, his fingers brushed her ankles, and she had to control an impulse to shiver. His fingers felt so warm and strong.

Then he took her hand again, and she felt herself returning his clasp. He led her across the lava whorls caused by boiling bubbles that left shapes like huge petrified flowers. Tide pools everywhere on the ledge were dotted with big black buttonlike sea creatures clinging to the sides. They made their way past several smaller spouts, which were eclipsed by their more famous big brother.

"It *is* a dragon," cried Susan when they were close to the large spout. "Look, there's his nostrils," she pointed to two holes in the rock. Stepping closer she held out her hand to feel the air rush up. "It's warm!" she cried in surprise.

"Well, what would you expect? It's a fire-breathing dragon, of course."

Then the horn spouted fifty feet into the air right in front of them and they ran back to the car, laughing all the way about the soaking they received. And even in the car Michael continued to hold her hand. Susan waged war within herself; but every time she looked at the man beside her she lost another battle.

Michael drove on through the beautiful Hanapepe Valley and stopped at the scenic overlook. They stood looking at the red clay cliffs on the other side of the green, green valley. The sky was a clear blue filled with fluffy white clouds, with no sign of the earlier dismalness of the day. A white water river ran along the bottom of the valley and on out to sea.

The breeze tossed Susan's hair, making it sparkle in the sun like cloth of gold. Michael's arm was around her shoulders. She felt so warmed, so protected, so at ease. His lips brushed her hair. She could feel his breath on her cheek.

She closed her eyes and leaned against his strong arm—melted against him in an overwhelming sensation of deliciousness.

Then reality came to her with storm clouds that obliterated the sun and laughter of the day. She pulled away. "No. Stop it, Michael. . . ." The angry words caught in her throat. She turned sharply and stumbled back to the car.

He reached out to open the door for her, but Susan stepped in front of him and jerked it open. She jumped into the passenger seat and slammed the door shut behind her.

Michael walked slowly around the car and got into his seat. He sat for a long time, just looking at her thoughtfully. Susan expected him to apologize, but he said nothing. The powerful engine of the little sports car purred into life and they drove off in silence. At the town of Wiamea they turned onto the canyon road. On each side of the car were breathtaking hedges of vivid bougainvillaea. The branches draped with masses of white, orange, deep burgundy, coral, gold, lavender, cerise, and fucshia blossoms. Susan had no idea the plant could produce such a riot of color. But the riot inside her own brain was far more compelling.

Suddenly she was no longer in a flashy sports car touring the Garden Island of Kauai with Michael Travis. She was back on the campus of Koinonia College. At least she could now laugh about the name. It translated love, fellowship, brotherhood—in her two years there she had never once encountered a hint of those qualities.

She had gone there reeling from the shock of her mother's sudden death, and the frightening discovery that she had been left penniless. Her Uncle Charles, married to her mother's late sister, had sent her there out of the goodness of his heart and a desire to dispatch his role of guardian painlessly. Instead of love and comfort she had been given rules, prejudices, and "thou-shalt-nots." She was told they were God's rules—whether they were or not she didn't try to discover for herself. After six months of struggling to earn her righteousness she abandoned it as impossible and decided to stay impious. Of course, she didn't try anything openly rebellious, but the day she came of age she packed her bags and left for San Francisco. A week later she was working days as a chambermaid at the Langford and spending her evenings studying public relations at hotel management school. Two years later she had her degree and a job as assistant-to-the-assistant in the Langford's PR department. But seven years and many promotions later she still hadn't forgotten the lessons learned at Koinonia College.

They had said they were Christians. . . . All that narrowness had been enforced in the name of Christianity. . . . Michael was president of a group of Christians. She shot a glance at him. At least he was a lot more fun to be with than those kids had been. He'd undoubtedly smiled more in the two days she'd known him than all the students on that campus together had smiled in the two years she'd been there.

So, either he was a different sort of Christian than they were, or he'd given up too but wouldn't admit it and was hanging on as a hypocrite. That certainly seemed the most likely. Lawyers were natural-born hypocrites—which led her to the next step. If he was a hypocrite about his religion, he was probably being a hypocrite about his apparent liking for her.

But then maybe he wasn't a hypocrite; maybe he

really was that narrow. It just wouldn't show as much on a man—they didn't have to follow strict dress codes anyway. But then, maybe . . .

Oh, why did she have to get mixed up in this! She looked out the car window through hot tears at the enormous gorge they were driving along, and tried to concentrate on the red clay bluffs and the silver line of river running through the floor of the crevice.

It seemed like hours since Michael had spoken to her, which was just fine—she didn't want him to talk. She wouldn't be able to believe anything he said anyway. But the air in the little car was becoming oppressive. It was as if there were an invisible shield between them. Suddenly a great surge of anger swept through her. She wanted to strike out and smash that shield and smash that smug, deceitful, insincere, sanctimonious, handsome, clever, charming—Pharisee sitting on the other side.

She worked herself into such a rage that she probably would have done something from the pure force of her feelings had Michael not suddenly stopped the car at a wide turnout and come around to open her door for her. He held out his hand to help her from the car, but she ignored it and struggled out by herself.

They walked side-by-side, but not touching, to the metal railing surrounding the lookout and stood for some time on the brink of the enormous mile-wide gorge. It was an awe-inspiring scene of red and green, bearing remarkable resemblance to the Grand Canyon. The passing clouds created ever-changing patterns, which lent further shading to the multicolored tones of lava strata cut by millions of years of erosion from the rainfall on lofty Mt. Wai'ale'ale. Fortunately there were no other tourists there at that moment.

Finally Michael turned to Susan. "Now, would you like to tell me what's wrong?" It was an open invitation, spoken without emotion or pressure. The counselor was offering his services.

She started to refuse but as she opened her mouth to speak the trite phrase, "There's nothing wrong," she was amazed to hear herself saying, "I don't like lawyers."

His response was a buoyant laugh. His reactions were a constant amazement to Susan. "What a relief—I was afraid it was something personal. I'll have to admit to knowing quite a few I don't care for myself. I believe we're quite generally notorious for being a very dull group." He turned toward her, suddenly serious, "But, Susan, I believe your prejudices are based on something more than boredom."

He was quiet, inviting her to talk, but not forcing. She nodded her head slowly, looking at the lava rock beneath her feet. "My father died before I was born—killed in the Suez as a member of a UN peacekeeping force. In the will he wrote before he went overseas, he established a trust for my mother, naming our faithful family lawyer as executor."

She spoke hesitantly with a note of bitterness in her voice, "For eighteen years the kindly Mr. John P. Wilcox, Esquire, kept my mother on a subsistence level allowance while she struggled and scraped and scrimped taking various part-time jobs and raising me."

"Of course she never questioned Mr. Wilcox. He was the fairy godfather who sent us a pittance of a check every month. When Mother died and I looked through our papers, I discovered that my father had left a reasonably comfortable estate including his lump sum veteran's benefits, but our Mr. Wilcox had charged the trust lavishly for his own expenses as executor. Charged it so lavishly that it was conveniently all gone. I didn't even have enough left for Mother's funeral expenses." She turned away from

Michael and away from the canyon, her back to the railing. The hardness in her heart prevented her saying anything more.

Michael nodded slowly, "Yes, I see. He expensed it to death. An all too easy technique I'm afraid. But didn't you realize you could have sued him?"

"Of course I did!" she flashed angrily. "I don't know how many lawyers I called and went to see. I lost count after six or seven, but do you think any attorney would take on a penniless client without payment in advance? And where was I to get that kind of money?"

"You could have filed a complaint with the Bar Association."

She gave a caustic laugh. "Mr. Wilcox was on the ethics committee of the Bar."

"Wow! No wonder you reacted so negatively to our association." He put his hands on her shoulders and turned her toward him. When she refused to look at him, he put a finger under her chin and tilted her head up so that she was forced to meet his gaze. "But, Susan, give us a chance. We aren't all like that. Let us show you before you convict and sentence the entire profession."

"I don't know. . . ." She didn't sound very hopeful, but she allowed Michael to keep his arm around her shoulders to guide her back to the car.

Driving down the steep, winding canyon road they were met at every turn with a breathtaking panoramic view of the glittering ocean over the tops of the trees; with glimpses of a narrow curving strip of golden sand edged with a white fringe of surf, and the sun shimmering on the blue water beyond, and of the red clay channel in the ocean where the river rushed out to sea bearing its load of iron-rich soil.

They still didn't talk much—as a matter of fact, the only conversation was when Michael stopped briefly to point out a pair of mountain goats on the canyon wall—but the tense, charged atmosphere that filled the car on the way up had evaporated. It was now comfortable, almost companionable.

They drove back through the Eucalyptus Avenue, the philodendron-wrapped tree trunks striping long dark shadows across the pale pavement like a zebra. And all too soon, Susan felt, they were back at the Langford.

They took the elevator to Susan's floor, but two women got in with them, so there was no conversation. Somewhat chagrined, Susan recognized the tall elderly woman with the gray hair piled high on her head as being the lady she had almost collided with in the lobby on her unfortunate first morning at work. When the door opened Susan started to get out. Michael's hand on her arm restrained her. "Wrong floor," he said as the ladies exited and the elevator continued on up another floor.

When it stopped a second time Susan stepped off the elevator and turned right. Again Michael's hand restrained her. "Wrong way," he grinned at her. "What do you do when you don't have a Seeing Eye dog along?"

"Well, obviously, I've managed." Her voice was flippant, but she made no attempt to shake his hand off her arm.

Three turns down the corridor, accompanied all the way by swaying palm trees so close they could have reached out and touched them, and they were at Susan's door. "Will an hour give you enough time?" he asked.

"Time for what?"

"To be ready for dinner. Our date was for the whole day, remember? Don't you think it's your professional responsibility to know what the competition offers in the way of dining opportunities, too?"

Susan laughed, "I'd love to see you in court—as long as you were on my side. Make it an hour and a half."

A long soak in hot bubbly water got rid of the last of the day's tensions. Susan brushed her hair in a golden froth and slipped into a light pink dress with long billowing sleeves that hung from her shoulders to a swirl of pleats. Her magenta shoes had spike heels, open at the back and only a few straps across the front.

Michael smiled appreciatively at her appearance and she had to admit she could find no fault with his either. He was wearing an ivory-colored suit. Even his shoes matched the color; Susan had never before known a man who dressed so well.

"Where are we going?" she asked as they left the parking lot.

"The Coconut Pa Ali," he replied. "It's a Victorian palace. Superb food and I think you'll like the blend of European and island decor."

Indeed Susan did like it. As soon as they stepped under the great thatched roof it was like stepping back a hundred years in history. The shiny black lacquer tables were surrounded by high-backed Empire chairs. Some tables were lighted by tall, many-branched candelabra, others by colorful Tiffany lamps. From the ceiling hung sculptured metal palm fronds with groups of light bulbs that resembled clusters of dates. Some of the tables were given semiprivacy by curtains made of strings of shiny black candlewood nuts and fat gold beads. It was to one of these tables that the waiter escorted Susan and Michael, lighting the candelabra before handing them large, tasseled menus.

The conversation was easy and relaxed as Susan and Michael nibbled on French fried artichoke hearts, which they dipped in little lotus flower bowls of thousand island dressing. Michael told Susan about his mother who lived alone in their family home in Seattle, about his younger brother, David, whom he was putting through Willamette Law School and hoped to take into partnership someday. He had just begun telling about his latest big case when the waiter brought their salads—hearts of palm and asparagus vinaigrette. The salad plates were garnished with orchids and after finding a hair pin in her evening bag Susan pinned the lavender blossoms in her hair over her left temple, island style.

"Go on, I want to hear about your case," she urged. That was funny—until a few hours ago the last thing in the world she would have wanted to listen to would have been a lawyer talking about his work.

"I represented a widow who had been defrauded of some very valuable real estate property by an attorney who was representing both her and a real estate development company wanting to build condominiums on it."

Susan made a face.

"Yes, I know what you're thinking," Michael nodded gravely, but his eyes were smiling at her. "Another shyster to add to your list. As a matter of fact he was. It took us five years of litigation to get him and the development company, but we did it. So you see, there is some justice."

"And how much did all this cost the poor widow?" Susan's old cynicism returned to her voice.

"A lot of mental anguish, I'm afraid, but the court awarded costs, so the other side had to pay her legal fees as well as give her the property and the condominiums they had built on it. She did very well."

"And I suppose her attorney did very well too?" She didn't really mean to be nasty—things just kept coming out that way.

"I had taken the case on a contingent fee. That meant I didn't get a thing until and if we won. Yes, I came out all right—that's one reason I'm able to take this vacation—but it was a gamble. Five years is a long time to wait to get paid."

"Wouldn't you have more professional success if you weren't so attached to this parochial Christian Lawyers thing? No matter how lofty their goals are," she added hastily.

"Well, I'm also on the board of the American Trial Lawyers Association," he said mildly.

She flushed. "I withdraw the objection, your Honor. I hope you realize you're destroying all my nice comfortable prejudices."

The rattle of the waiter coming through the beaded curtain prevented Michael from replying more than a simple, "I certainly hope so." The mahi mahi in cream sauce with shrimp, scallops, and mushrooms was sufficiently succulent to claim their attention.

The meal ended with guava sherbet and Darjeeling tea. Susan added a squeeze of lemon juice and just a bit of honey to the tea in her cup. She took a sip, then sat back with a sigh. "That's exquisite," she said dreamily. "I love tea, it's one of life's rare pleasures. But I seldom drink it."

"Why not?"

"Not enough time. You can gulp coffee. Tea must be sipped. I'd rather not have it at all than to have to rush."

While Susan was savoring her second cup of tea, the lights came up on a small platform and a Hawaiian man sang a selection of island love songs. He was accompanied by two young men playing native instruments. A beautiful olive-skinned girl with huge dark eyes and long black hair danced rhythmically to the music. The girl was wearing a long, oyster white, flowing gown of a gauzelike fabric, which swayed gracefully with her as she moved, its long full sleeves rippling like fans from her uplifted arms. Susan couldn't recall the last time she felt so relaxed.

When the show was over, she and Michael walked out into the balmy night air, the soft music from the palace following them. Stars twinkled brightly through the branches of the royal palms high overhead. . . . Susan made no objection when Michael put his arm around her and held her securely. She was sure she felt his lips brush her hair lightly, and it sent a thrill through her. She would not have pulled away as she had only that morning. But he went no further.

When Susan got back to her room the message light was blinking on her telephone. With a sigh she obediently rang the front desk. "Yes, Miss Jamison, you are to call a Mr. Nichols in San Francisco."

"Thank you," Susan replied wearily. She glanced at her clock. It would be after three o'clock in San Francisco now. Much too late to call Josh.

She went to bed with the sliding glass door onto her lanai open and slept soundly to the lull of the rolling surf.

CHAPTER 3

AS SOON AS SHE AWOKE. SUSAN ran out on her lanai and gave a little cry of joy to see that the sky was a clear azure blue, promising a sun-filled day with Michael. She dressed carefully in a white sundress with a wide off-the-shoulder ruffle and a skirt of tiered ruffles. Each ruffle was banded by a pastel ribbon: lavender, blue, pink, yellow. Her sandals had a strap of each color, too. She carried a white straw bag and a wide, floppy brimmed straw hat to wear in case her hair and delicate skin should need protection against the tropical sun later.

She decided to go down early and look over the things on her desk before Michael arrived, but just as her door closed behind her she heard her telephone ringing. Quickly locating the key in her oversized bag, Susan returned to her room.

"Problems here, Susan," Ted barked into the phone without preliminaries. "Get down here fast."

"Yes, sir." She felt as if she should salute.

"Close the door," he said as she entered his office.

As she obediently closed the door she realized the patrician-looking silver-haired woman she had seen around the hotel was seated in the leather chair next to Ted's desk and her liveried chauffeur was trying to comfort her in a case of what appeared to be incipient hysterics.

Ted presented Susan to Mrs. Agatha Irving. "Mrs. Irving was checking out this morning when it was discovered that her jewels are missing from the hotel safe—not to mention yesterday's receipts," he added wryly.

Susan gasped, then forced herself to think clearly. Quick-wittedness was a prime requisite for her job and she had to arrange her responsibilities in order of priority: Keep the guests happy, supervise security, protect the hotel with the media. . . .

"I want you to understand that I hold the hotel directly responsible for this," the matron said in haughty tones unmitigated by her gentle southern dialect.

"You've called hotel security?" Susan asked Ted.

Before he could answer Mrs. Irving spoke scornfully, "Hotel security? I want the police! I want that man charged! If the thief escapes because of your shilly-shallying I shall have my attorneys sue you—the hotel and you personally," and looking at Susan she added, "both of you."

"Now, Mrs. Irving," Susan tried her most soothing tones, "we have an excellent security force here—highly trained and efficient. I'm sure that a person of your sensibilities doesn't want this splashed across the papers. If we can handle the situation internally it will be much simpler."

"Simpler for your public relations," she snorted. "Will you call the police, sir? Or shall I call the police *and* my attorney? I have no desire to miss my flight this morning; I have social obligations at home."

Ted and Susan exchanged glances and he resignedly picked up the telephone. While Ted was speaking to the police sergeant Mrs. Irving cut in again, "And tell him to bring a squad car to haul that night clerk off in!"

"Night clerk?" Susan asked when Ted hung up the phone.

Ted nodded grimly, "Kele was on duty. The jewels were there when the day clerk put the receipts in before Kele began work. He seems to have been the only person known to be behind the desk last night."

Susan's mind reeled with horror. If this was an inside job, committed by a Langford employee, the publicity would be a disaster. She had to keep it out of the papers. And then an even worse thought struck her. Kele was Lani's fiancé. "Ted, does Lani know?"

Ted nodded succinctly, "I thought it best to tell her before she heard rumors."

"Right," Susan agreed, then her professional training forced her to add, "but no one else need know. I'll put out the story that Kele went home sick." Mrs. Irving started to protest, but Susan quelled her, "The quieter we keep this the less interference there will be with the investigation from curiosity seekers, Mrs. Irving. I'm sure that's what you'd want." Susan started for the door, "Ring me when the police arrive; I'm going to find Lani."

Susan thought hard, trying to recall the Hawaiian man she always saw at the front desk when she came in late. The image was blurred—she had spoken to him no more than three or four times. She remembered the thick black hair that waved over his forehead—unusual because most Polynesian men had straight hair—and she remembered a mole on his left cheek that moved up and down in an intriguing way when he smiled—which he did most of the time. But Kele wouldn't be smiling now.

43

Nor was Lani. She sat with her head on her desk, her shoulders shaking with sobs. Susan laid a hand on the thick black hair that fell like a heavy veil around the girl's bent shoulders. "Lani, try not to cry. I'm sure everything will be all right." Susan didn't know Kele, but she knew Lani and she couldn't imagine the girl would fall in love with a criminal.

"I know he didn't do it," Lani said, making an effort to stifle her sobs. "But I'm sure he'll be arrested. I'm so afraid. If only I could help him." Her disjointed speech was drowned in a gulping sob, "We're to be married this summer."

"Try not to worry, Lani." Susan searched her mind for something to say, something to do to help her friend. But she was lost.

Hotel policy was one thing, but this involved legalistics . . . and she had spent years avoiding any connection with legal authorities. Then softly, like the gentle waves she had seen lapping at the crystal beach, an idea soothed her frenzied thoughts. "Lani," she said, "I think I know someone who might be able to help." Michael's calm assurance, level gray eyes, and firm hand came to her mind like a solace. "Wait here. I'll see what I can do."

Lani tried to say thank you, but her sobs choked her.

Michael apparently could see the trouble on Susan's face as she hurried to him across the lobby. "What's the matter? You don't have to cancel today do you?" he asked, his steady voice according the assurance she needed.

"Oh, Michael, the most awful thing has happened." She explained quickly as she led the way to Lani's office. Lani was sitting just as Susan left her, her head bowed, her shoulders shaking. Susan removed the soggy tissue from Lani's hand and gave her a fresh one.

"Now, then, Lani, Susan told me about your problem. I want you to take about three deep breaths, dry your eyes, and try to tell me everything again very calmly. Susan, why don't you go get her a cup of good hot coffee."

To Susan's amazement, the composure in Michael's voice transferred itself to Lani, and the girl quit sobbing almost immediately. By the time Susan returned with the coffee, Lani was listening to Michael's advice calmly and dry-eyed.

"It wouldn't be wise for me to talk to Kele myself because I'm not licensed in the islands, and anything he would say to me might not be privileged. So you should go to him. Tell him that if he's guilty the money and jewels should turn up immediately in a place that won't be traceable to him. If he does that, I think I can get the hotel and Mrs. Irving not to press charges. On the other hand, if he's not guilty he should adopt an aggressive stance of trying to help the investigation."

Lani actually smiled as she nodded. "Yes, it sounds reasonable when you explain it. Thank you so much." She set her coffee cup down and reached for a pencil on her desk. "Now tell me again. I'll write it all down so I'll get it right."

Michael patiently repeated his directions and Lani wrote down every word.

Susan answered the ring of Lani's phone, "Thank you, Ted. I'll be right there." She replaced the receiver and started for the door, "I'll be back as soon as I can; the police are here."

At that word Lani's composure dissolved. "Police! What if he's arrested!"

"Lani," Michael said firmly, "they can't do that without probable cause. Opportunity isn't probable cause."

Susan opened the door to Ted's office in time to

hear the police sergeant growling at Mrs. Irving, "Lady, we've got to have *probable cause*. You want us to arrest your driver here? He was in the hotel, too." Susan looked over her shoulder to see that even Lani managed a smile.

Susan spoke quietly to the officer who was only too happy to turn away from Mrs. Irving's demands. "I'm sure Mr. Rawlings has told you that he and I and our security guards will do anything we can to assist you." The policeman nodded. "But we would appreciate anything you could do to keep this quiet from other guests and employees as much as possible and especially out of the press, of course."

"I understand. We'll do our best. If we treat it as routine at headquarters it's unlikely the news services will pick it up—we're pretty small potatoes on the out islands."

"Ah, just one of the rewards of not being in metropolitan San Francisco." Susan relaxed visibly, her major responsibility to the hotel taken care of. There was nothing else she could do now. Kele was not going to be arrested, and the police would handle the investigation. She turned to Ted, "I had a rather full day scheduled. . . ."

"Run along. I think we have everything under control here." Ted waved her out.

Susan entered Lani's office with a swirl of her ruffled skirt. Michael smiled at her from across the room, rising to meet her. "The police will be leaving soon," she said. "Without Kele."

Quickly and gracefully, as Lani did everything, she rose from her chair and threw her arms around Michael's neck and kissed him soundly on each cheek. "Mahalo, oh mahalo—thank you so much," she beamed at him.

Michael smiled at her and gave her a brotherly hug. "I'm glad I could help. We'll be back this evening and you can give us a report then."

"You were terrific with her," Susan said, once they were outside. "I want to thank you too."

"The same way?" Michael asked mischievously.

"Not in the middle of the parking lot," she replied lightly, getting into his Mazda RX-7.

"Right," he agreed. "I'll collect later. Want some breakfast?"

Susan shook her head, "In all the excitement I guess I lost my appetite."

They drove for some time, exulting in the beauty of the sun shining on the rugged mountains with their flocking of green vegetation to the left; the blue, blue Pacific to the right; and the gentler blue sky overhead with fleecy white clouds like a mirror image of the white surf in the water.

The drive forever remained in Susan's memory as a collage of brilliant images: Little houses with banks of tropical flowers almost covering them . . . green rolling fields dotted with horses and clumps of trees . . . a flock of graceful, delicate white egrets . . . a little cemetery nestled in a green hollow . . . haul-cane roads criss-crossing the highway . . . palm trees lining the view of cloud-topped mountains in the distance . . . cattle grazing in pastures overlooking the Pacific . . . a grove of papaya trees sheltering tightly-packed clusters of green and yellow fruit beneath their umbrella of giant serrated leaves.

They left the main road and drove past a diminutive lava rock church with stained glass windows and a wooden cross on top, surrounded by a clipped green lawn. A tiny cemetery nestled by its side under swaying palms.

"The influence of the missionaries is still evident everywhere on the island," Michael remarked casually as they rode past the doll-like building.

Susan wanted to comment on how some missionaries' narrowness and bigotry had spoiled much of the island's heritage, but held back as she recalled that there was hardly a church on the island without a school or hospital operating right next door. Besides, it was too nice a day to spoil with talk of religion. "Mmm," she said.

Past the village they left the pavement for a red clay road, which became narrower and narrower and leafy foliage reached out to sweep the sides of the car. A puddle of water from recent rains splashed up, looking like tomato soup. "Oh, just think what your car's going to look like," Susan cried.

But Michael didn't seem worried. "We're almost there. I think you'll agree it's worth it."

"Where are we going?"

"Kilauea light station," he replied. "It's one of my favorite spots on the island." And when the car rounded the last curve of the narrow road and came to rest before a breathtaking panorama, Susan immediately saw why it was so special.

They climbed out of the car and walked slowly across the dirt road to stand near the edge of the cliff. Far below them spread the turquoise water with wind-tossed whitecaps that rushed forward to crash and churn in billows of foam on the rocks. To their left was a lava cliff carpeted with green velvet and crowned with a red-roofed, white lighthouse. Birds sang above them in the filagreed Ironwood pines, the long, tufted needles swaying in the breeze like graceful hula dancers. Around the cove to their right, large white seabirds nested on the side of the cliffs like giant marshmallows.

The leaf-filtered sun was warm on Susan's head and tall grasses rustled at her feet. The breeze caressed her cheeks. She filled her lungs with the fresh cleanness around her, breathing in its purity, exhaling her cynicism and frustrations.

Michael stood quietly beside her, respectful of her

privacy. After several minutes of solitude Susan looked at him and smiled. He then put his arm around her gently and drew her to him.

His fingers tightened around her waist, drawing her closer. She made no protest when his lips slid from her tousled hair to the smoothness of her soft cheek. "Susan," he murmured, turning her to him.

The crashing surf thundered with the beating of their hearts. As the timeless waves rolled beneath them he held her in timelessness. She had never known a kiss could be like this. After an eternity that passed like a moment he released possession of her mouth and she slumped against him.

A bird flew by with a raucous cry. Susan started. They weren't the only living creatures on this enchanted island. "On to Bali Ha'i," Michael said softly, his lips near her ear, as he guided her back to the car.

Susan sat in a trance. She knew she should be fighting this—this feeling he brought out in her, but it was far too delicious. She didn't want her life complicated by this man, but at the moment she couldn't fight him.

They drove for some time in warm, soft silence. Susan smiled at Michael when he turned his head and caught her studying him. "Getting hungry yet?" he asked.

She nodded.

"Think you can hold out for a restaurant?" he asked with a grin. "Those are Scrambled Eggs bushes along the road, but I'm afraid the name is purely esthetic."

Susan turned to look at the bushes covered with clusters of yolk-colored flowers. "They do look like scrambled eggs," she laughed. "But I can wait. Is it far?"

As she spoke, a roadsign came into view. "Hanalei," she repeated, reading the sign. "Where have I heard of that before?" Her brow furrowed as she tried to recall the elusive strain.

Michael smiled and hummed a few bars of a familiar melody.

"Of course," she cried with delight, "Puff the Magic Dragon." He joined her in singing. ". . . lived by the sea and frolicked in the autumn breeze on a beach at Hanalei," they paraphrased, ending in laughter.

It was one of my favorite songs as a kid," Michael said. "I always looked for Puff when we came here."

"Ever see him?" Susan asked with perfect solemnity.

"No." Michael shook his head sadly. "Probably because it wasn't autumn."

"He must be related to the dragon at Spouting Horn," Susan commented.

"I'll bet that's Puff himself, hibernating until there are autumn breezes to frolic in," Michael suggested.

Susan was mystified. How could anyone so sophisticated and so incisive also be so much fun and indulge in such nonsense?

They stopped for lunch at a resort set among the verdant greenery of the hillside overlooking a crescent bay. The restaurant was perched on the edge of the slope with one side open to the view. Michael led Susan to a small table next to the open veranda and pulled her chair out for her. Island music floated softly in the background. A jungle of Bird of Paradise and bougainvillaea tangled with the other plants ringing the terrace while in front of them, spread like a living mural, the rugged, cloud-crested mountains rose from the gentle blue bay, ever washing the sands at their feet.

Michael pointed to the mist-draped mountain framing the bay, "There it is—that's Bali Ha'i—where the sky meets the sea." Susan gazed in wonder at the magic of the mountain, not realizing she was holding her breath. The words of the song from *South Pacific* ran through her head. As if in answer, the music in the room played softly, the words coming gently to her ears . . . words of people who live on lonely islands, lost people who long for something more, some other place where hopes and dreams flourish. In the song, the island, Bali Ha'i, held the answer to the dreamers longing.

But that was a song. What about her? Was she a lonely island, lost in the middle of a foggy sea? What part did this tantalizing man have to do with the special island, the deep longing that called her mysteriously?

As she sipped her hot, mellow, Darjeeling tea she looked up and found Michael's eyes on her. Their gazes held each other. She set her cup back in its saucer with a clatter. His hands came across the table to meet hers.

It wasn't evening and the room wasn't crowded, but the moment was enchanted. "You will see your true love," the song repeated in her mind and over the stereo speakers.

No! she told herself sharply and withdrew her hand. She would never go through again what she had suffered at college: Ostracism for using her own mind, denial of her own personality, slavish subservience to a dogmatic code. It had all been fine at first— wonderful even, she'd have to admit, when she first became a Christian at the church she and her mother attended. She was sixteen then and for a long time the world held a special glow for her—then she went to Koinonia College. . . .

A boat with billowing white sail skimmed across the bay far below them. Little brown birds with pale golden chests hopped in from the terrace garden and pecked at the crumbs under deserted tables. The soft music continued and Michael was still smiling at her, but the moment was no longer enchanted. Why did the most attractive man she had ever met have to be a Christian? She could put up with his being a lawyer—maybe—but she could never submit to living a life of sanctimonious cant and regulated pretense again. For one niggling moment the thought flashed through her mind: *But what if it could be like it was earlier? Before the rules?* But that wasn't possible, she had learned something from her "college education."

She thought about asking Michael to take her back to the hotel now. Goodness knew she had enough work to do. And she could use Lani as an excuse. What if the girl needed her help? But then she recalled that this really was business—part of her job to get to know the island, she reminded herself. She smiled at the flimsiness of the excuse, but when Michael asked her if she was ready to go on she nodded.

They drove through a narrow, lush valley, the road winding through intense greenery with the sun shining on the wispy, silver clouds frothing around the top of Bali Ha'i above them, on past taro paddies and houses built on tall poles like stilts. The mountains ahead of them were pinnacled and turreted like a medieval castle and beribboned with silver threads of water-falls. Single lane bridges spanned most of the rivers, but sometimes they drove right through little streams rushing down the mountain and across the road in their hurry to get to the ocean. The jungle closed in around them and vines hung from tree branches over their heads.

A now-familiar Hawaiian warrior roadsign announced their arrival at a cave. "Want to explore?" Michael invited, and Susan was sure she saw Tom Sawyer looking at her out of those shining gray eyes.

"Sure," she said, jumping out of the car door he was holding for her.

As they approached the great lava cliff that over-
ung the road with vegetation growing all over its
ough surface, Michael took her hand and led the way
nto the low, wide mouth of the cave. Immediately
hey were in a different world—this strange habitat
ould easily be on a distant planet. The sound of
ripping, splashing water echoed all around them in
he cool semidarkness of the lava tube. The wet sand
oor was dotted with small pools of water dripping
hrough the porous base of the mountain overhead.

They walked slowly deeper into the cave. Looking
ack toward the long, low entrance was like looking
hrough a curtain of waterfall to the sun-bright clarity
f blue and green and brown beyond. Light from the
ntrance shone on drops dancing in the pools, each
alling droplet splashing a miniature crystal fountain.

At the back of the cave the roof sloped down to the
and floor as if a giant bowl had been turned over
hem. "Maybe it's another dragon and we're inside
is head," Michael teased as they looked through the
lackness to the long, low slit of the opening.

"It does look like a giant eye, just open a squint,"
Susan agreed. "What if he goes to sleep? Will we be
rapped here until he opens his eye again?"

"It's too wet in here to build a fire like Pinocchio
id inside Monstro, so we'd better get out while we
an." More of Michael's delicious nonsense.

Susan ran for the opening, then blinked fiercely as
hey exited from the gloom of the cave, and dug in her
ag for her sunglasses. "Is there more?" asked Susan
s she took her seat in the car. "It looks like we're
bout to the end of the road."

Michael smiled, "I've saved the best for last."

And a short time later when they were standing at
he edge of Lumahai Beach, Susan had to agree that
his, indeed, was the best. The water was almost
green as it washed with an edging of white lace on the

pale sand, and the luxurious foliage from the jungle grew right to the edge of the beach, giving a feeling of sheltered intimacy.

"So this is where they filmed *South Pacific*," Susan said looking around with wonder in her eyes. "And to think it's still all unspoiled."

"Yes, wouldn't it be a sacrilege to put up condominiums here?"

Susan stood at the edge of the sand, mesmerized by the rustling boughs over her head and the rolling water beyond her feet. She was almost afraid to desecrate that spotless beach by walking on it. Michael stood behind her, his hands on her shoulders. Somehow they felt so right—so strong and so warm and yes—so exciting. Susan felt little tremors shock the length of her body from where his hands rested on bare skin.

"Did you bring your swimming suit?" he asked.

Susan gave a little laugh, "Of course. A woman doesn't carry a purse the size of this one without her complete wardrobe in it."

"Good," he said with a smile. "Ladies to the right, men to the left."

Only a few feet into the dense growth and Susan had the privacy of a dressing room. She had brought her best suit. It had cost her three days' salary in San Francisco, but she wasn't sorry. It was one piece of soft white fabric. On the top was a design of scarlet and amethyst chrysanthemums, each of their delicate petals outlined in metallic gold, like a piece of cloisonné jewelry. The halter back tied behind her neck with a double gold cord. Over the suit she slipped a beach cover with a border of the same exotic cloisonné work.

Michael was on the beach waiting for her. He looked marvelous in white trunks that emphasized the perfection of his golden tan. Susan had realized he as well built, but standing there on the beach in his swimming suit, the sun shining on him, he was stunning. He turned toward her, and she simply couldn't help herself—she ran to him. He held out his arms and caught her, lifting her above his head as if she were weightless.

"Race you to the water," he said, setting her on her feet. It wasn't much of a contest. Susan arrived at the water's edge laughing and out of breath, several paces behind Michael who only jogged to keep ahead of her.

"You cad, a gentleman would have let me win," she laughed.

"Oh, sorry," he teased. "I thought that was considered condescending chauvinism or something nowadays."

She didn't reply, but turned to frolic in the frothy tide instead.

"Do you want to swim?" Michael asked, helping her out of the beach cover. "There are strong offshore currents here, so we can't go out far."

"Fine with me. I'm not a strong swimmer, but the water looks heavenly."

And it was heavenly—warm and buoyant, the surf rocking them gently. To her surprise Susan was able to swim a good part of the distance across the bay with frequent intervals of turning over to float on her back. Michael swam strongly near her, diving down and swimming farther off when she stopped to rest.

"Getting tired?" he asked when he swam back to her after one such time.

"A little," she admitted.

So they swam lazily back to shore and spread out the thick beach towels Michael had produced from the trunk of the car, and lay on the golden beach beneath the golden sun.

"Do you have any sun block lotion in that cavernous bag of yours?" he asked. Susan nodded and

55

produced a plastic bottle. He took it from her and began smoothing the creamy white lotion over he shoulders and down her bare back. "I would hate fo that beautiful skin to get burned," he said.

The lotion was cold, but the touch of his hand burnt like fire. She controlled a desire to tremble.

Then, suddenly, she was angry. She was angry with Michael for making her feel like that. She was angry with herself for feeling like that. She was with Josh for never making her feel like that.

Michael stretched his long body on his towel next to her. He was so close she could sense his breathing and feel his presence even though their bodies weren' touching. She pulled her big hat over her head, turned her face away and pretended to doze. The pretense worked so well that the next thing she felt was a feathery touch on her back. Her sleepy mind separated Michael's deep voice from the roar of the sea. and she sat up suddenly.

"Hey, Sleeping Beauty, time to head back."

Her eyes met his look, and she remembered she was mad at him—even if her drowsy brain couldn' quite remember why. She jumped to her feet, slipped on her beach cover, and gathered her things.

Back at the hotel, Michael asked where they would find Lani. "I told her we'd see her this evening."

Susan looked guilty. She had been so wrapped up in her own experiences she had forgotten all about Lani. "I don't suppose she works this late, but maybe we can find her home address in her office."

When they arrived at Lani's office, however, they were surprised to find that she was still there, just sitting at her desk and staring blankly. When she saw them she gave a little cry and jumped up. "Oh, Miss Jamison, Mr. Michael, I am so glad you've come." There were no tears, but she began trembling violently

56

Michael took both her hands firmly and led her to a chair. "Now, Lani, tell us what's happened." Just as it did that morning, his calm voice acted like a sedative on her. She controlled her shaking and was able to answer, "Kele has disappeared. I went to his apartment when he didn't answer my phone calls. He was gone. I looked around. A few of his clothes seem to be gone, too. I couldn't be sure."

"Oh, Lani, I'm so sorry." Susan was at Lani's side with a comforting arm around the miserable girl. "Do you think that means he's guilty?" Susan asked Michael, looking at him over Lani's bowed head.

"Not necessarily. Innocent until proven guilty is for us to remember as well as for the courts. People do unpredictable things in situations like this. Lani, I have a friend who's a private detective in Honolulu. He owes me a favor. Shall I ask him to come over and help us?"

Lani raised her head, an almost hopeful look on her face. "Oh, yes. If you think that is the right thing to do. I must see Kele. I must talk to him, no matter what."

"Now that's settled," Michael declared, "the next thing is to get you settled. Can we take you home? Do you have someone to stay with you? Have you had anything to eat all day?"

Lani blinked and looked at them as if she were trying to remember. "I live with my sister in Kapa'a. She should be home from work in a hour or so. I guess I haven't eaten, I . . . I can't think."

"Right," Michael nodded. "Susan, you take her to your room and you ladies get freshened up for dinner while I make some phone calls. We'll see that Lani has a good meal before we take her home to her sister."

Susan didn't even object to Michael's giving orders. Both women were glad to have someone take charge

57

of the situation. They each showered quickly and after Lani had re-tied her ankle length pareau, the island dress that could be worn in about seventeen different ways, and brushed her glorious long black hair and pinned a fresh blossom in it, she felt enough better to give Susan a bright smile.

"Now try to enjoy your dinner and not worry," Susan said as they went down in the elevator. "Michael will take care of everything." *If only Michael could take care of my problems*, she thought wryly, *instead of causing them—or in fact, being my problem.*

When Susan had left the beach earlier that day she had entertained no thoughts of dining with Michael that night. But she could hardly abandon Lani, so here she was in the exclusive restaurant on the top floor of the Langford Kauai. They sat on the deeply padded and tufted seats and looked out at the torches in the garden far below them and the lights flickering on Nawiliwili Bay beyond. The glimmers outside were repeated inside by strings of tiny white bulbs shining brightly in banks of plants along the walls and between the stair-stepped rows of tables.

Conversation was light as both Susan and Michael endeavored to keep Lani talking about island history and customs. She was happy to comply. "There were five Kings named Kamehameha," Lani said, indicating the portraits hanging on the walls behind them. "The first was known as The Great—he ruled for about fifty years after Captain Cook rediscovered the Sandwich Islands, as he called them. King Kamehameha The Great conquered many island chiefs and joined the islands into the United Kingdom of Hawaii. Kauai was never conquered, though. We accepted him by treaty. . . ." Lani seemed to relax and shake off her problems as she talked and the meal progressed pleasantly.

When Michael took Susan back to her room after they had given Lani to the care of her sister, Susan was evasive about plans for tomorrow. "I really can't say, Michael. I've been gone for two whole days and Thursday we have our 'Lei Aloho o Kuhio,' with the Royal Court present and everything. I really have an awful lot left to arrange for that. I don't even think the centerpieces have been ordered yet," she finished lamely.

"That's fine. I'll need to spend the morning on the phone with my detective friend, James. It's been two days since I checked in with the office, and I haven't even called Heather at all yet. Can you have your centerpieces ordered by one o'clock?"

"Well, maybe. But I really can't say for sure. Something may come up," she hedged.

"You mean, maybe you'll think of something by then?" he laughed, giving her a penetrating look. "What size shoes do you wear?"

She was so startled by his strange question while her mind was still asking, *Who's Heather?* that she replied, "Seven," before she realized what she had done.

"Good. See you at one." And he was gone. He hadn't even given her the pleasure of turning away from a goodnight kiss. What an infuriating man!

In spite of the quick shower she took before dinner, Susan undressed and headed for the bathroom. She usually preferred the luxury of a long, deep, bubble bath, but the hotel shower heads were equipped with a massage unit and tonight she wanted the feel of the turbulent pounding water to match her mood. She turned the faucets on hot at full-blast pressure. As the water rushed out with startling force on her back and shoulders she slowly felt her tense muscles relax and the knots inside her untie themselves.

It was only a kiss, she told herself. *That was hours*

ago and the lighthouse was miles away, you should have forgotten the whole thing long ago—Michael undoubtedly has. You're just lonesome, overwhelmed by the newness of everything. But no matter how hard she argued, deep inside she knew that no kiss had ever been like Michael's. No man she had ever met had been like Michael.

CHAPTER 4

THE NEXT MORNING THERE WAS nothing new on the robbery investigation, and Kele had not returned to his room. Susan worked furiously at her desk, attacking one pile of unfiled correspondence after another. The centerpieces for the gala were ordered with a simple phone call to the florist. The printer delivered the "Aloha" newsletters, and she arranged with housekeeping to have one delivered to each room.

"Ready to let me take you away from all this?"

The deep voice made Susan jump. She had been so intent on her work that she lost all track of time and even managed to shut Michael out of her mind for a short time. Her desk was almost clear. She really didn't have any excuse to refuse, and she would like to get out of the office for a while. She smiled in surrender.

"Can your friend help Lani?" Susan asked after she had obediently gone to her room for her swimming suit as Michael directed her.

"It may take some time, but James Aukaina is very good at his job."

"What's the 'favor' he owed you?"

Michael shrugged, "We've worked together before."

"You're hedging. . . ."

He smiled, "Well, I didn't want Lani to worry about expenses. But really, he had a suspect show up in Seattle once and I was able to give him a hand. He'd done some process serving on Oahu for me before that. Nothing very dramatic."

"Okay, next question. Why did you want to know my shoe size?"

They were now in the car, headed for a south shore beach. "Snorkeling equipment." Michael pointed to the back seat with a jerk of his head. "Wouldn't want your fins to fall off."

"Snorkeling!" Susan sounded alarmed. "I told you yesterday I'm not a strong swimmer. Don't you have to be certified and everything for that?"

He laughed. "You're thinking of scuba diving. Snorkeling is a kids' sport, but it's great. Trust me— you'll love it."

She very much doubted it, but Michael never asked—he just told. And he had told her she was to enjoy it.

When they arrived at the beach house Michael decided to leave the wet suits in the car. "It's such a warm day I don't think we'll need them."

When she emerged from the dressing room, he was waiting for her.

"I feel so conspicuous without a suntan," she said, comparing her alabaster skin to his bronzed body.

"Don't worry, white woman is a delicacy here."

"Oh," she shivered. "Horrid. You make it sound as if I'm to be eaten." She refused to meet the glint in his eye.

They walked to the water's edge and Michael helped her with her fins, face mask, and air tube. "Do you feel it forming a vacuum when you breathe in?" he asked, adjusting the strap on her mask. She nodded. "Good. Now, you hold the rubber end of the tube between your teeth and keep your lips tight around it. The hardest part is remembering not to talk. Everyone forgets the first time and gets a great big glub for his effort."

Susan looked doubtful. "Are you really sure about this?"

"Yes, I'm sure. I wouldn't take you into anything dangerous, Susan." The gray eyes looked at her levelly and communicated confidence to her.

They walked knee deep into the water. "Now just lay down and the water will hold you up," he directed. "Don't try to swim with your arms, that will only tire you out. Just a little kick of your fins will move you through the water. If you want to say something, tug at my hand, and we'll come up to talk. If you see a shell you want, point to it, and I'll dive down and get it for you. But don't you touch anything. If you don't know what's what you can really get stung. Ready?"

"I'm not very athletic," she held back.

"I'll hold your hand all the time. And we'll never be in water over your head."

"Promise?"

"I promise," he said solemnly and adjusted his own mask.

She nodded and lay face down in the water. To her amazement, it did support her. Michael's strong hand held hers firmly. With little flips of her ankles she propelled herself through the water, holding tightly to Michael. She could feel an energy between their hands, like dancers in a pas de deux or championship pairs ice skaters.

The sun filtered through the water in pale golden shafts. The sound of her own breathing through the snorkel tube was loud in her ears, and she could hear a faint sound of splashing from her fins. Suddenly a big fish passed in front of them sending up a shower of silver bubbles. She squeezed Michael's hand and pointed excitedly. He returned her message with two quick squeezes. A school of small silver fish passed underneath them, making little sand storms where their fins scraped the bottom of the bay.

Susan relaxed; the beauty and excitement were thrilling. Rocked by waves, they floated over a green and lavender coral reef dotted with spiny, violet and black sea urchins living in little holes in the coral. Round, brown sea cucumbers lazed on the sandy sea bottom looking like uncooked sausages. A colorful fat shell caught her attention and she pointed to it. Michael nodded, let go of her hand, and dived down to pick it up. He surfaced with the plump purple shell in his hand and they both stood up to examine the treasure.

"A Sea Biscuit," Michael said, as pleased as she was. "I haven't seen one of these since I was a kid. This is a beautiful specimen. They are quite fragile and don't often make it this close to shore without getting crushed." He put the prize in a small net bag he wore attached to the belt of his trunks.

"Want to go for more?" he asked.

"Oh, yes! I love it!" Susan felt she could never get enough of that underwater enchantment.

"Sure you aren't tired?"

"Not a bit. Come on," she urged.

They lay down again in the warm water. Every few feet that they swam the panorama changed. A school of silver blue fish darted in front of them. Yellow, black, and white striped angel fish glided by with their graceful fins undulating in the water. Susan got so excited over a neon-bright red, white, and blue fish she forgot the prohibition against talking. When the first drops of salt water hit her tongue she quickly closed her mouth and blew out the tube as Michael had instructed. Then she squeezed his hand hard and pointed. He squeezed back and pointed, too, to let her know he had seen the beauty.

Long slim pencil fish dashed in and out of their field of vision. Susan was delighted with a tiny brown fish covered with bright blue polka dots, and a school of bright red fish with big black eyes. And then an oddly shaped pale blue fish with a yellow nose and spots took her attention.

They were floating just a few feet above another coral reef, the abundance of its beauty unlike anything Susan had ever before seen or imagined. *It's wonderful. Thank you God*, she said, completely overcome by its awe-inspiring magnificence. Then, horrified by the realization of what she had done, she brought her knees down sharply and threw her head up in defiance.

A sharp pain stung her knees, but she ignored it in her confusion over the act of betrayal her mind had committed. She had prayed! How could she have prayed when she knew very well there was no God? But then, hadn't she been blaming God all along for her troubles—taking her father, taking her mother, letting the lawyer cheat her, sending her to that horrible school? How could she blame Someone who didn't exist?

"Coral cuts can be very nasty," Michael said when they had surfaced, pushing his mask up on his head. "I think we'd better get you in."

Susan shivered, but Michael couldn't know it wasn't from cold.

"You've had enough for your first day. Look," he pointed to the other side of the curved cove. "Can you believe you swam clear across there?"

Susan stared. She really couldn't believe it. It had taken no exertion at all.

"Come on now." Michael helped her put her mask back on and took her hand to swim toward shore. Twice on the way in he let go of her hand and dived for shells to put in his bag.

Susan emerged on the beach dizzy from the motion of the water. Michael held her close to him until she got her equilibrium, then led her to the sun-warmed sand. He wrapped her in a thick terry cloth towel he had left on the beach and offered her a smaller one for her hair, which she wrapped around her head like a turban. She sat there, tingling and enthralled by the activity and the beauty she had experienced.

Michael brought them glasses of fresh pineapple-orange juice from a beach stand and they sipped it slowly, admiring the treasures from the bag: The pudgy fat sea biscuit, a spiny purple sea urchin, a bright orange-red shell that looked like a golf ball with sticks poking out all over it that Michael identified as a sea pencil, and three smooth, speckled cowry shells. "The native Hawaiians used these as money," Michael told her, laying out the cowries.

"But now I want to take a look at that scrape of yours." He examined her bloodied knee. "Does it still sting?"

She nodded.

"Be right back," he jumped to his feet.

"Got a first aid kit in the car?"

"Better than that," he replied over his shoulders as he jogged off across the beach.

He returned in a few minutes with a piece of dull green cactus leaf. It had prickles along its sides and a sticky juice oozing out where he broke it off. "Aloe Vera," he announced. "It's got everything—iodine to prevent infection and vitamin E to speed healing and prevent scarring." He dabbed the juice on her cuts. They quit stinging immediately.

"Amazing," she said. "Does that stuff just grow wild here?"

He nodded, "I noticed a big plant by the roadside when we drove in."

Michael stretched his full length beside her and the sun glistened on his skin. Susan sat rigid. Her heart was doing flip-flops and she felt flushed and angry. Angry at her own confusion—confusion about Michael; confusion about God. And every time she glanced at the man lying relaxed beside her, her confusion increased.

He was so fine. He was so honorable. He was such fun to be with. And he represented everything she had turned her back on. The only man who could perturb her with his fascination was causing all her carefully erected defenses to crumble. And she didn't know what to do about it. Worse—she didn't even know what she wanted to do about it.

"Better get this salt water washed off before it begins to burn," Michael said at last. At the sound of his voice she jumped. She had been lost in her thoughts, supposing him to be asleep.

Back in the beach house Susan showered the briny water off her tingling body and shampooed her hair. She rubbed her body vigorously with a thick terry towel and emerged pink and glowing in her lime green sundress.

"You don't have to go back to the hotel before dinner, do you?" Michael asked a few minutes later. "I thought we'd have dinner on this side of the island."

"That's fine, but I didn't bring my blow dryer," Susan replied, tossing her damp tresses. So they tucked their bags and the shells into his car and walked in the gardens beside the beach until her hair dried, the warm tropical breeze working better than any electrical dryer. When she combed through her

67

golden locks the natural waves fell softly around her face like the halo of a renaissance angel on a Christmas card. Michael picked two white spider lilies from a wild bush and she pinned them in her hair native style.

Michael had made dinner reservations for them at an old plantation house converted into a restaurant. Susan never ceased to be amazed at his skills of organization. This was an area in which she was no slouch and she was deeply impressed by someone whose proficiency matched her own. She would hardly like to admit that they might even surpass hers.

They went into the gracious old house and were seated by the open windows. Susan relaxed. Her tensions eased, and her mind picked up the threads of her tangled thoughts on the beach. Why was she always so on guard with him? He made no secret of what he stood for, but he never made any attempt to preach to her or force his beliefs on her. So why did she feel so uncomfortable?

"You're very contemplative tonight," Michael said after several minutes of relaxed silence. "I hope you'll forgive my asking, but it's a natural question and I don't know any way to find out but to ask—why is it you're still single? You understand I'm not complaining," his eyes twinkled at her.

"You go first," she challenged. "Seems it's an even greater accomplishment in your case."

"You mean because I've maintained the condition longer?" he laughed. "I suppose thirty-three is a rather alarming age for the single status." He shrugged, "I guess I just never found anyone I wanted to spend the rest of my life with, and I sure wasn't going to try it on any terms less than absolute certainty. I've had enough professional opportunities to observe the disasters of divorce—even those that start out with assurance that they'll remain civil-

68

ized. . . ." He shuddered, then gave Susan a long, level look that brought her heart right up to her throat. For a moment she thought he was going to say more, but then he grinned at her—which did nothing to help her heart return to its normal position. "Your turn."

She gave him a mischievous smile. "Well, there was Johnny Culver who lived next door to us when I was six years old; he was my first love. When I was in the sixth grade I fell head-over-heels for a cowboy on TV named Russell something-or-other. In junior high it was an English rock group—"

"The *whole* group?"

"It had to be that way, I couldn't stand to break any of their hearts by playing favorites."

"Very considerate of you—fickle, maybe—but considerate."

She paused before becoming serious. "But to be fair, I'd better tell you about Phillip. We were together a lot in the teen group at church, then went to Bible college together." Michael's eyebrows shot up at that, but he didn't say anything. "We had a sort of understanding for quite awhile." She took a sip from her glass of water.

"And?"

"And then I walked out on the whole bag—college, Phillip, and faith." Again she was quiet for a moment, then forced a small smile, "Can you believe it? He was preparing for the ministry—narrow escape for both of us."

"I'd like to hear more about that part of your life, Susan. I was sure there was something, but I didn't want to pry."

"Maybe sometime," she tossed her hair with a flip of her head. "The deal was to tell about old flames, not a complete autobiography. Don't they have any waiters in this place? I'm starving."

As if waiting for his cue, a waiter in a short white

jacket with a towel over his arm appeared to take their orders.

Susan ordered seafood crepes hollandaise from the Light Dinners side of the menu and Michael had a delicate mushroom quiche in a puff pastry crust served on a ti leaf. They ate leisurely. And after dinner they walked slowly back to the car through torch-lit gardens, the pale, curving path a ribbon of silver in the moonlight.

But even after she was in bed she still couldn't find an adequate explanation for not telling Michael about Josh.

CHAPTER 5

A JANGLING RING CUT THROUGH the lulling sound of the surf. Then Susan realized she had been asleep. She had been dreaming, but she couldn't remember what. She had a vaguely euphoric feeling, though, so it must have been pleasant.

With a groan she rolled over and pushed in the stem of her alarm clock. The ringing continued. It finally penetrated her consciousness that the phone was ringing. She reached farther over on her night stand and grabbed the receiver. The room was dark. It must be the middle of the night. What could be wrong? Lani? Maybe the police had arrested Kele. With a voice thick from sleep and unsteady from apprehension she spoke, "Hello?"

"Susan, at last. I'd almost given up."

She sighed. "Josh, do you know what time it is here?"

"Oh, yeah. Sorry about that. But Susan, what's going on over there? Why haven't you written? You haven't returned my calls. You aren't even at your

71

desk during the day. And you are out all evening—every evening."

"Look, I told you before, I'm busy. I'm not at my desk because I have ten million things to see to as well as getting acquainted with the island."

"Getting acquainted with the island?" he sounded accusing.

"It's part of my job. I have to arrange sightseeing tours and things. You know perfectly well I did that all the time in San Francisco."

"And all night, too?" The third degree continued.

"It so happens I was *trying* to sleep tonight. But, yes, I am getting acquainted with other restaurants in the evenings, too."

"And just who else are you getting acquainted with?"

Josh sounded more like a prosecuting attorney than the rising young executive he was. And she didn't like it. She didn't like the tone of his voice. She didn't like the fact that she was guilty of the things he suspected. A stony silence communicated her rising temper over the phone.

"Susie, I'm sorry," Josh backed off. "I know you're working hard. That's just the point. You work too hard. When are you going to come home and marry me and quit all that?"

"Josh, I don't know."

"That's what you always say, Susie. Now listen, I'm getting tired of it. Are you going to marry me or not?"

"Now you listen yourself. You woke me out of a very sound sleep. I can hardly talk, let alone think, and you expect me to plan my wedding?"

"Look, I'm not the one that's hung up on marriage—that's you, remember. I'll be delighted to cut the red tape and have you just move in with me if you can't cope with planning a wedding."

72

"Josh! You know better than that. We've been over this at least three dozen times."

"I know—you've never gotten away from your puritan upbringing, and I'm willing to do it your way. I'm just reminding you it's your requirement, not mine. But you still didn't answer my question. Yes or no?"

"I suppose so," she said weakly.

"You *suppose* so!" The menacing sound of his voice made her glad for all the miles of ocean between them. She had the feeling he would throttle her if he could get his hands on her. "Susan, you hand in your resignation in the morning. Type it out and sign it and give it to them—do you hear? Give them two weeks—a month if you have to. But I want something definite. This has gone on too long, and I won't stand for any more of it. Do you hear me?"

"Yes, Josh, I hear you."

He took that for acquiescence to his orders and changed his tack. "Susie, I love you. You know what I say is for you too. That's what I want, you know, what's best for both of us."

"Yes, Josh," she said like an obedient child who had been chastened by a sharp reprimand.

"That's great, honey. First thing in the morning, now. Remember."

"Good night, Josh."

At least he hadn't forced her to say she loved him, she thought as she returned the phone to its cradle. But what had she said? *Had* she promised to resign and go home and marry him? She hoped not. She sure hadn't meant to, but she would have said anything to get him to stop shouting at her. She felt like swearing as she tore the covers off and jammed her feet into her slippers. As if Michael Travis weren't enough to cope with, now she had this.

She had only slept for about three hours, but it was

73

no use going back to bed in her present state. She pulled on a pair of jeans and a sweater, changed her fuzzy slippers for a pair of tennis shoes and made her way out to the beach.

Down by the water the air was damp and chilly. That was good; maybe it would clear her brain a bit. She wished she could just open her mouth wide and let the fresh air blow clear through. She felt as if her mind needed a good housecleaning. Not just her mind—her whole life. She hated untidy drawers. She hated a cluttered desk. She hated a disordered life. And right now hers must deserve some kind of garbage collectors award for confusion, turmoil, and agitation.

She didn't know how far she walked. She had long passed the beach front of the Langford and the coconut grove beyond it. She had walked across the sands surrounding a little bay lined with condominiums, and was probably somewhere on a deserted strip of public beach when she finally stopped. Funny, she mused, how the rhythm of walking could help get one's whole system back in time with the rhythm of the universe.

The lush plant and animal life of the island lived in abundant harmony with the natural order; the sea rolled in timeless, relentless tides with the moon; but she was tossed and buffeted like a speck of sand on the beach by every wind that blew through her life. She had nothing to anchor to.

She sat on the cool sand and picked up a handful of the smooth grains, letting them sift through her fingers like the hours of her days. That was what she needed, she thought, an anchor to hold fast. Josh? He was certainly unbending enough. Maybe his domineering was what she needed. If she gave in and did what he said, she'd be securely sheltered. *Or smothered?* a small voice from another part of her mind asked.

And even as she hardened her mind to reject the thought, Michael was before her. She thought of how he calmed Lani's storms, and knew he could do the same for the tempests in her own life. But even if she would give in to his kisses and the life he seemed to be offering, even Michael didn't seem like enough.

She was going to have to straighten out her own life, her own goals, her own ideals before she could anchor to another person. The thought was over-whelmingly depressing. She couldn't cope with this herself, and yet she knew no one else could do it for her.

The stars and moon were hidden under a thin cloud that made the world a very dark place. Susan sat huddled on the beach for a long time, her head resting on her bent knees, her arms hugging her legs. At length she rose and brushed the sand off her jeans. The breeze made her shiver. She decided to walk back by the sheltering bushes that grew along the island side of the beach.

It was even darker here and she had to pay attention to where she walked to avoid tripping over rough ground or walking into a small bush. It was good to be required to concentrate on physical movement—it kept her mind off harder things. She stepped to the right to walk around a bush.

Suddenly a scream caught in her throat. The bush moved. She froze, her heart thumping against her chest. Then she started to run, but the man that could no longer be mistaken for a bush put out his arm and caught her wrist. It was like a terrible recurring nightmare where she tried to run from deadly peril but was unable to move. Pain stabbed her hand from the wrench of his grip, but she hardly felt it compared to the panic inside of her. What an idiot she had been to wander out alone! She wasn't even sure where she was. She had been warned about incidents of assault on the island. *White woman is a delicacy*, she remembered ominously.

Just then the moon broke through its thin cover and cast a dim light on her assailant's wavy hair. "Be quiet," he ordered. "Just be quiet. I won't hurt you." Then she saw the mole on his cheek.

"Kele!" she cried. "Where have you been? Lani is simply frantic."

He jumped back in surprise. "Who are you?" he demanded.

Susan told him quickly of all that had happened at the hotel the last two days. But she refrained from asking the question uppermost in her mind. Michael or his detective friend could ask Kele if he did it. She wasn't going to tackle that alone on an empty beach.

"Please come back and talk to Lani," she pleaded. "We can help you."

Kele seemed acquiescent but her problem was deciding where he should go. She could hardly smuggle him into her room in the hotel, and the police were watching his apartment, and no doubt, Lani's house too. Michael could tell her what to do.

That was it. She must get Michael. She persuaded Kele to come back to the hotel with her, but he would not leave the safety of the sheltering bushes. So they made their way slowly through the tropical growth until they could see the lights of the hotel grounds just ahead of them.

"You aren't going to call the police!" He grabbed her arm roughly and swung her around to face him.

"No, Kele. You can trust me. But you must promise to wait here till I get back. Running will only make it worse—you must realize that."

He nodded.

Susan made her way swiftly and silently past the pool, across the hotel grounds, and up to her room. The clock by the phone said 4:32 as she pushed the buttons for Michael's room.

76

He answered on the third ring. "This is Michael Travis." He didn't even sound sleepy.

The resonant timbre of his voice coming down the wire was strangely exciting and calming at the same time.

"Michael, I've found Kele. He's down at the beach. Can you come now?"

He didn't waste time asking why or how, he just said, "Five minutes. Where on the beach?"

"The cabana."

"Right."

"And Michael . . . ," she hesitated.

"Yes?"

"Thank you."

"Sure thing."

"Of course it was stupid to run," Kele was saying to them a few minutes later, huddled in the warm blanket and gulping the instant coffee Susan had smuggled from her room. "But I was so scared. I knew I'd be the first one they'd suspect. I have a juvenile record, nothing too terrible, just joy riding, but it won't look good."

Michael shook his head reassuringly, "I doubt that record still exists. It was probably stricken from the files by now if you've had no further problems."

Kele looked momentarily relieved, then went on, "But who else was there? Besides, I am guilty."

Susan gasped and tears sprang to her eyes, thinking of the gentle Lani. "Oh, no, Kele . . . ," she began, but Michael silenced her with a raised hand.

"Not guilty of what they think, of course," Kele hurried on. "But guilty of giving the thief an opportunity. You see, I went to sleep at the desk. It's strictly forbidden—for obviously good reasons—and I'm sure to lose my job. Work isn't easy to find on the island and with Lani and me planning to get married this summer . . ." He shook his head, his eyes on the bare cement floor of the cabana.

"Yes, I see," Michael said calmly. "Jim will be here in the morning." Kele nodded. They had already told him about the detective from Honolulu whom Michael had called in to help. "Knowing what you've told us will be a big help to him. Now, Kele, the only thing for you to do is to turn yourself in. Remaining a fugitive will be no help to your case."

"No!" Kele jumped up so sharply he spilled the coffee remaining in his styrofoam cup. "You don't understand. They'll put me in a cage. I can't stand to be locked up!" He had a frenzied look in his eyes like a trapped wild animal. His nostrils flared and his body quivered.

For an awful moment Susan held her breath, afraid Kele might do something totally unreasonable like bolting out the door or attacking them. But Michael quietly put a calming hand on the frightened man's shoulder, "No, Kele. It'll be all right. We'll get you the best attorney in the islands, and I'll go your bail."

Kele slumped to his seat.

At nine o'clock the next morning Susan was at her desk. She had an excruciating headache. She was already on her third cup of coffee—and she didn't even like coffee. The events of the night kept replaying themselves in her head like an exceptionally vivid movie. It was impossible to believe they had really happened: Josh's demanding phone call, the surrealistic meeting with Kele on the beach, Michael taking the submissive Kele to the police, her own extended phone call to a tearful Lani. And now she was back in her office as if none of it had happened— except for the pain that was threatening to split her head in two and the dark circles under her eyes.

"Miss Jamison," a white-coated polynesian boy

burst breathlessly into her office, "Mr. Rawlings said to come at once. The senior citizens tour busses just pulled in."

"What? They weren't scheduled until this afternoon!"

"Yes, Miss. Mr. Rawlings said you'll have to take care of them until their rooms can be prepared."

Susan grabbed her clip board with a groan. "Did you say buss*es*?"

"Yes, Miss Jamison—three of them."

Her head throbbed as she hurried toward the lobby. *Three busses at forty passengers a bus. What in the world am I going to do with a hundred and twenty senior citizens for four hours?*

By the time she got to the lobby it had been engulfed by a wave of brightly flowered shirts over rotund stomachs each with a camera strap across it, and polyester pantsuits with limp leis hanging below well-coifed gray hair. Porters were hauling a mountain of luggage to an unused room where it would be locked up until housekeeping could ready sixty rooms whose occupants hadn't even checked out of them yet.

Susan rang the bell on the front desk for attention and pasted on her brightest smile. "Aloha! Welcome to the Langford Kauai." Even as she spoke, her mind was formulating a plan. "Since we have the pleasure of greeting you a few hours earlier than we expected—and we can certainly understand your eagerness to get to our beautiful island—I'm going to ask you to get back on your buses, and I will personally escort you on a tour of our lovely botanical gardens." There were murmurs of pleasure from the crowd and several of the men checked the film in their camera cases. "And since your rooms aren't ready for occupancy yet, the admission to the gardens will be compliments of the Langford Kauai."

The colorful wave receded from the lobby, and Susan turned quickly to the desk clerk. "Have Lani arrange with the kitchen for a buffet luncheon to be set up by the pool when we get back." The man jotted down her instructions. "And if Mr. Travis returns tell him where I've gone." Susan grabbed a tourist brochure about the gardens from a rack near the door and went out to board the front bus.

Fortunately the driver needed no instructions on how to get to the gardens as he turned the bus to the south. The drive was long enough for Susan to read the leaflet thoroughly en route, although she was wishing desperately that Michael had taken her there. At least this experience certainly gave validity to his arguments about the need for her to know the island.

Susan saw from her quick study that the garden was really a series of six different gardens and as soon as they were off the busses she organized the oriental guides that accompanied the group to have each take twenty people to one of the different gardens. They were to rotate in a clockwise direction and hopefully thereby avoid swamping the gardens or trampling on one another's toes.

The group was indefatigably cheerful, for which Susan was thankful. "What pretty hair you have, my dear," she heard over and over again from smiling ladies. "You're doing such a good job," several assured her with a pat on her arm. "And you're so young, too." Over and over again she posed, smiling obediently, into a camera wielded by one of the men. "I wonder if I could get you to stand over by that tree with my wife for a minute?" She began to wonder how many times she had been asked that. "Now smile pretty, girls," and the wife would titter. At least Susan was glad she was wearing her bright yellow dress with a softly gathered skirt. The dress would photograph well even if her tired eyes and forced smile didn't.

At last the guides marshaled their forces and led them off to their assigned starting points, following the maps provided by the garden management. Susan took a deep breath and let it out slowly. It was the first chance she'd had to think since the emergency struck. Now she wondered what was happening with Kele. Michael had gone to the airport in Lihue to meet James Aukaina and get him started on the case. She certainly hoped he could prove Kele's innocence. She was proud of the way Lani had taken the news—even showing up for work this morning in spite of her red, swollen eyes. Well, Susan decided, now that she was here she might as well see the gardens herself. Following her map, she set out for the floral knoll. The hedge of hibiscus shrubs immediately took Susan's attention. She had seen the large exotic blossoms in Hawaiian girls' hair, and even the smallest yards exhibited several colorful bushes of Hawaii's state flower, but she had never seen anything like the display before her.

She turned to walk back the length of the curved hedgerow. There were many things to see in the garden, but she was in no hurry to leave the splendor before her. She walked slowly, feeling the sun on her head and the smooth grass under her lightweight shoes. Chatter and laughter from the tour groups floated to her from every side, but for the moment she was alone in this spot.

"Ah, there she is, the loveliest flower in the garden." At the sound of the deep male voice Susan turned with a smile and just in time checked the impulse to fling herself into the speaker's arms.

"Michael! What's happened? How did you find me? How's Kele? Is James here?"

"Whoa, one at a time," he laughed, offering her his arm. "Jim arrived right on schedule. Everything's fine. And when I heard at the hotel what'd happened I

81

thought you might need some help. But I can see you have it under control."

Susan took his arm. "Yes, thank goodness you'd mentioned the gardens earlier. Everyone seems to be delighted."

Michael led her toward the palm court as they talked. "Jim is already at work on the investigation. He's very efficient and very thorough—as well as using the latest in scientific paraphernalia for his work—I think we can hope for results soon."

They paused to look up at a stately Queen Palm, its plumed fronds resembling a giant feather duster against the clear blue island sky. "And Kele?" Susan asked.

"I filled him up on sausage, pancakes, and rice. You know, the locals eat mounds of rice with everything. Then I took him to his apartment with firm orders to get some sleep—he hadn't had more than a few naps since the whole mess began."

"So he's out free?"

Michael nodded and drew her attention to a giant fan growing in front of them. "Look, this is called the Traveler's Tree. See how its branches grow in stair steps? Each one forms a cup that will trap as much as a quart of water, so the traveler can always be sure of finding a drink."

"Amazing," Susan said, surveying the tree. "But how did you do it?"

"I didn't do it. The tree was wholly God's idea."

Susan laughed, "Silly. I mean, how did you get Kele out?"

"Just had my bank wire the bail to the court. Very efficiently accomplished with one phone call. Waiting for the bank to open was the only delay."

"But, Michael, that must have been an enormous sum of money. And you hardly know Kele."

He smiled at her and patted her hand that was

through his arm. "One thing about my profession—we get to know all types. I think I'm a pretty good judge of character. Don't worry about it now, just relax and enjoy the gardens. I wanted to bring you here anyway, so this is great."

Susan couldn't believe palm trees came in so many sizes and shapes. There was a Chinese fan palm that could have been used to fan an ancient Eastern potentate; a windmill palm, with its fronds spread in a shape that would tempt Don Quixote to a joust; a triangle palm with a three-sided trunk; a bottle palm with a trunk indeed shaped like a giant bottle, just right for housing a genie.

It soon became a private game with them to avoid the clumps of tour groups making their way from garden to garden. Susan and Michael giggled like children as they moved quickly, and not too obviously, they hoped, ahead of the invading mass that rapidly filled the sunken garden. The game combined the secretive skills of a good hide-and-seek game with the guilty pleasure for Susan of feeling she really ought to be with the hotel guests.

They stood before a giant White Bird of Paradise bush with flowers looking like feathered heads sticking out all over it. "I can't believe it," Susan gasped, I thought Bird of Paradise were just little things in flower beds.

"Yes, but the white variety is a tree." Michael led her along the path. "Now if you want to see a big tree, how about this?"

They stood before an immense Banyon tree, its spreading horizontal branches reaching out more than a thousand feet with aerial roots growing from them to the ground. "It's as big as an apartment house," Susan said, shaking her head in wonder.

"Uh oh, time to move on." Michael moved quickly toward the house garden as they heard the voice of a guide behind them pointing out a Philippine persimmon plant accompanied by appropriate oohs and aahs and camera clicks.

They stopped before an Angel Trumpet plant hung with large white horn-shaped blooms that "would certainly be useful for staging a Christmas pageant," as Michael commented, and moved on to a Green Jade Vine. Susan was so busy admiring the long clusters of luminescent turquoise, slipper-shaped blossoms hanging from the vine that she didn't hear the sight-seeing party approaching.

"To the rain forest," Michael said in a stage whisper and they were off at a near run, laughing all the way.

It was damp, quiet, and secluded in the jungle. Its silence broken only by the chattering and chirping of birds. Even footsteps were muffled by the moist, heavy air, and soft dirt path. Susan felt as if she had been transported suddenly to another world—Africa? South America? India? That was it—she carefully scanned the next banyon tree she found, sure that Mowgli must be asleep somewhere on its branches.

She walked ahead of Michael, lost deep in her fantasy—so deep that she walked right off the path and would have landed in a very gooey looking mud puddle if Michael hadn't put out his arm to restrain her in time.

"Watch it," he said, his voice alight with amusement.

Susan was embarrassed by her absent-mindedness, but that feeling was quickly forgotten as a much stronger one overcame her. Michael pulled her to him. She could feel his breath on her cheek and smell his clean after shave mingling with the heavy jungle scents. The stillness of the jungle enclosed them. The bird sounds seemed strangely distant as his lips came close.

"Fred, where are you? I can't find the path," a shrill voice penetrated their intimacy.

"We're over here. Take the path to the left," a voice that was apparently Fred's answered.

"But I can't find it. Come get me," the female voice wailed.

Now their oriental guide appeared on the path below Susan and Michael, "What's the matter? Are you sinking?" he called good-naturedly to his stray charge.

Laughing quietly, Susan and Michael fled to the upper path and out of the jungle into the sunlight. The world returned to normal, but Susan was left with a vague sense of loss.

CHAPTER 6

SUSAN AWOKE THE NEXT MORNING, aggravated to discover it was barely seven-thirty. It was Sunday morning, her one day to sleep in, so what was she doing awake? She rolled over, pulled the covers up to her ears, and told herself to relax and go back to sleep.

Ten minutes later she realized she was lying quite rigid—hardly conducive to drifting into somnolence. She turned onto her back, arms at her side, and began counting slowly backwards from five, concentrating on relaxing a different part of her body on each count. She had read a book on progressive relaxation years ago and found the technique to be invaluable—almost foolproof for getting to sleep.

But not this time. By the time she reached "one" and should have been slipping into a peaceful slumber, she found every muscle in her body was tensed. With a groan she got out of bed and reached for her robe. Well, she'd use the time luxuriously on herself anyway: do her hair, have a facial, a delicious bubble

87

bath, a manicure, and pedicure. The promise of such self-indulgence was as good as sleeping in—almost.

She was nearly at her bathroom door when she heard the strangest sound in her room. She turned and looked, trying to locate the source. It couldn't be her alarm clock, she hadn't set it last night. The TV and radio weren't on. Finally she saw it. . . . What on earth was that pillow doing over her telephone?

Then she remembered. The message light had been flashing its insistent red eye at her when she came in last night after a late supper by the pool with Michael. The last thing she had wanted was to have more ultimatums shouted at her by Josh, so she just buried the whole thing with an oversized, dacron-filled bolster. Now it was struggling valiantly to make itself heard from beneath the muffle.

Susan extracted the red-eyed monster from its covering.

"Hello."

Sure enough, it was Josh with yet another of his "What's-going-on-there?" harangues, which she handled as calmly as she could until the conversation suddenly took an unexpected turn:

"Be honest with me, Susie. Are you in love?"

She gasped as the words hit her. "Yes I am," she blurted out. "I really am!" Amazement and wonder filled her.

Then horror. What had she said? And to Josh, of all people! But how could he possibly have guessed? She had barely been beginning to guess herself. Her face was hot, her hands sweaty, and her heart was pounding so loudly she was sure Josh could hear it over the phone.

"Well then, what are you shilly-shallying around about? I love you and you love me. So come home and marry me. It's as simple as that."

Susan let her breath out in a slow stream. What irony. He thought she was in love with him.

"No, Josh, it isn't that simple. You don't understand."

"Oh, I know. Your job again. But you've given them notice, haven't you?"

Silence.

"Susan! I told you to give them notice three days ago! What is the matter with you?"

A knock sounded at her door like a blessed reprieve.

"I have to go now, Josh. Your phone bill must be astronomical. I'll write when I have something definite to tell you. Good-bye now."

She hung up quickly before he had a chance to argue with her.

Hastily doing the buttons on her robe, Susan went to the door. "Who's there?"

"Room service."

"Room service? I didn't order anything." She unlocked the door, but did not undo the chain. Peering out she saw that indeed it was room service.

She opened the door and the white jacketed boy wheeled in a small table covered with a white linen cloth, laden with a basket of flaky fresh croissants, pats of pale yellow butter on ice, a silver bowl of marmalade, and a steaming pot of her favorite Darjeeling tea with lemon and honey. In the center of the table was a bud vase with two heart-shaped red anthurium and a card. She picked up the card with her heart in her throat and read, "Good morning, Michael."

She directed the waiter to wheel the table onto her lanai. It was a glorious morning, she decided. She sipped her tea and nibbled at the light French rolls and reveled in the freshness of the morning. It had rained during the night, but the meneheune had outdone themselves in clearing the clouds away and scrubbing the world clean. The surf was rolling its bass notes and the birds were warbling in soprano. Susan's heart sang with them.

Michael's breakfast tray came to her as something of a peace offering. They hadn't exactly quarreled, but their parting last night was less than harmonious. He invited her to go to church with him this morning. Her instinctive reaction was a sharp retort that she could find better things to do with a Sunday morning than to spend it in a stuffy room filled with mindless hypocrites.

To her surprise, instead of flaring back in defense, Michael smiled at her (she could still see the twinkle in his eyes), and replied that he knew of at least one mindless hypocrite who would miss her. He then said that as he would be spending the afternoon on the investigation with Jim and Kele he wouldn't see her until evening, but he'd take her to the torch light ceremony at the Coco Palms at dusk.

Then before she even had time to accept, he had pulled her into his arms and engulfed her with a kiss that left her with a tight, choking ecstasy that threatened to drown her. Even now on her lanai in the morning sunlight she needed only to close her eyes to feel again the rapture it had stirred in her.

By the time Susan finished her breakfast the air was warm and the thought of a swim was inviting. She decided to postpone her beauty salon activities until later. She hadn't even used the hotel pool yet and this was a perfect opportunity. She slipped quickly into her suit, grabbed her towel, sun oil, and book and went to the pool.

The water was lovely and fresh, the sun making little golden dappled patterns like mosaic on the blue bottom of the pool. She swam a languid side stroke under the arched bridge that spanned the waterway between pools and then rolled over on her back to float lazily in the aqua water, looking up at lofty palm trees spreading their dark green fronds against the lucent blue sky.

There were few other swimmers in the pool this morning. Susan spread her arms and swam a few feet of backstroke to take her closer to the tumbling waterfall. She wondered how close she could get to it without getting a face full of water. It was a rude shock when she suddenly found herself tangling arms and legs with another swimmer.

She tried to say she was sorry but got a mouth full of water for her efforts as both swimmers struggled to right themselves. As if by common consent they both swam to the edge of the pool, heaved themselves out, and sat there dripping and laughing.

"I am sorry. I'm afraid it was all my fault. I wasn't watching where I was going. I guess I thought I had the whole pool to myself," Susan said to the young woman beside her.

"That's all right, honey. Ah wasn't watching either, Ah'm afraid," the girl replied in a slow southern drawl.

Susan was surprised to see that the girl had even less suntan than Susan did, in spite of the fact that the southerner had dark hair, so would presumably tan easily. "Have you just come to Kauai?" Susan asked.

"Ah've been here about three weeks, but Ah don't get much time in the sun. Ah work at the hotel," she replied.

"Oh, well, so do I," Susan responded. "I work in public relations, where do you work?"

"Ah'm in catering," the girl said, looking around nervously.

Susan noticed her discomfiture and wondered if lower echelon staff were not permitted free use of the facilities when off duty. She decided to change the subject and try to put the girl at ease.

"My name's Susan and I'm new here, too. I'm from San Francisco. Where are you from?"

"Ah'm from Georgia," the girl replied, losing none of her uneasiness. "Mah name's Anne Marie," she added quickly.

"I'm happy to know you, Anne Marie. What did you do before you joined the Langford?" It was part of Susan's job to be able to converse with anybody and put them at ease. This girl, however, was not one of her successes.

"Ah think Ah'll swim some more," she said, slipping back into the water. "Bye." And she splashed away, leaving a mystified Susan sitting by the pool.

Susan toweled off, rubbed coconut oil sun lotion on her body, and stretched out in a lounge chair with her book. Susan liked romantic novels written a generation ago by such authors as Elizabeth Goudge and D. E. Stevenson. Today she was well into Elsweth Thane's *From This Day Forward*. It was a beautiful love story; she felt as much in love with the hero as the heroine was. And now the heroine, Liz, was fighting a desperate battle against overwhelming odds to save the life of her lover who had been trapped by a landslide in a Mexican jungle. Susan kept telling herself that it was silly to think the hero might die, and yet she couldn't really trust this author—she *had* killed one of Susan's favorite heroes in another book.

The rain was beating blindingly in Liz's eyes, her feet kept slipping in the newly upturned ground, and she had lost all sense of direction. Susan was completely lost in the story, choking on her swollen throat. *Help her*, she pleaded, *Don't let him die*.

She was into the middle of the next paragraph when she realized what she had done. This was too much! That was the second time she'd caught herself praying in a week. And it was all Michael's fault. No matter what his kisses did to her, she wasn't going to give in to this mythological nonsense.

She flung the book down, unaware that it landed in a puddle made by a dripping swimmer, and plunged into the pool, barely taking enough thought to pull her sunglasses off first. She swam furiously, flailing against the water and using much more energy in her strokes than casual swimming required. But she wasn't concerned about economy of motion; she wanted release from emotion.

When she finally emerged from the pool, after having done countless laps, she was breathing heavily and her arms and legs felt weak. But she had worked off a lot of steam and felt she could cope with an evening in Michael's company—even knowing he would bring his faith with him.

After her promised afternoon of prodigal luxury, she met Michael with a glow. She could see that the effect of her romantic, sheer, white dress with a large pink organdy flower at the waist was not lost on her escort. Her hair swirled on top of her head in a soft knot with long tendrils curling around her ears and down her neck. She wore tiny pearl earrings and an alluring floral perfume. The effect was definitely one of moonlight and orchids.

In the parking lot Michael bent down and took a tiny nibble of her neck. It sent shivers running up and down her spine. Only Susan knew how little it took from this man to undo her composure. She walked quickly to the car and stood by the passenger door, waiting for him to open it.

"Wrong car," he said, taking her arm to guide her further down the row.

"This island seems to propagate little blue cars," she said in self defense.

They drove inside the thickly hedged grounds of the Coco Palms and parked. Their walk to the restaurant took them through a maze of waterways, thatched buildings, and jungle gardens.

"This was the setting for an Elvis Presley movie in the '50's," Michael commented as he led her across a little bridge spanning yet another strip of water.

Susan laughed. "Well, I'm afraid that was a bit before my time. I was born in '57."

"My goodness, you *are* a child! I didn't realize. . . ." Michael said with a shake of his head.

"What's the matter, afraid you'll be accused of cradle robbing?"

He laughed. "Hardly that. But you do have a poise beyond your tender years."

"Well, thank you, sir. Life does that to one, you know."

"To some people, yes. Others don't learn from it. Some very old people never really mature—they just shrivel."

"I pride myself on being a fast learner. I try never to make the same mistake twice."

"That's a good policy—have the courage to make a new mistake. Goodness knows there's enough of them to be made. Why get in a rut?"

The conversation was light and they were both laughing. But Susan had a feeling there had been some real philosophy there. She'd think about it when she was alone.

"Are all these lagoons natural?" Susan asked, looking at the beautiful green and blue area they were walking through.

"They were built by Queen Liliuokalani as fish ponds. Mullet for the royal table were kept here in fresh water to remove the salt from their flesh."

"How interesting! So mullet are both fresh and salt water fish?"

"Yes. The queen was a brilliant, well-educated woman who married a Yugoslavian nobleman. I guess the taste for freshwater fish was just one of the European tastes she acquired."

"Wasn't she the last Hawaiian royalty?"

He nodded. "It's a rather unhappy story, I'm afraid. Just a few months after she began her reign her prince consort died. Her island economy suffered because of a U.S. law ending the reciprocity treaty. There was dissension in the kingdom. When the Queen tried to proclaim a new constitution her cabinet refused to sign. A mass meeting was held, attended largely by non-natives, and American marines gave support to the dissenters. The Queen feared bloodshed, so she abdicated."

"And then?" Susan prodded, intent on his account of island history.

"The Queen was arrested on charges of treason and held prisoner in the palace until she was granted a conditional pardon."

Susan shook her head. "Stories of the passing of the old order are always sad. I know change has to come, but sometimes one longs for the ways that are lost."

They walked silently on across Queen Liliuokalani's grounds and entered the thatched interior of the restaurant. They were seated at a table along the wall that was open from table height up. The lagoon ran directly below them and the sound of the gently lapping water mingled with the soft strains of island music being played inside.

The waiter brought a basket of crisp, wafer-thin Armenian bread coated with sesame seeds. Susan broke off a piece with a tiny snap and spread it thinly with sweet unsalted butter. She sat nibbling at the tasty morsel, listening to the sounds around her and watching the lights dance in the lagoon.

She took a deep breath and smiled.

"Happy?" Michael asked.

She nodded and smiled again, too thoroughly relaxed even to answer in words. She wondered briefly why it was that she could get so worked up and confused as she'd been this afternoon at the pool when she was alone, and then everything seemed so easy when she was with Michael. *Probably because I can't think at all when I'm with him*, she told herself.

While they were eating their tropical fruit cups Susan asked, "How did it go this afternoon? Did you find anything to help Kele?"

"We're not sure, but Jim has some ideas. Unfortunately it's too long after the fact for the super-scientific stuff he loves, like analyzing the fibers of the carpet; and the police didn't find any fingerprints except those that should have been there—day clerk's, Ted's, Kele's; but we all agree that it seems strange that Kele could have slept so soundly sitting at the desk that someone could have broken into the safe in the room just behind him."

"What are you suggesting? Do you think Kele's lying?" Susan looked worried.

"No, not that. I fully believe his story. It seems more likely that someone drugged him. But we can't figure out how. If we knew how, we'd probably know who, and then it should be an easy step from there to the thief."

"Did he eat or drink anything that evening?"

"Just a cup of coffee."

"That should have kept him awake."

"That's exactly the point."

"Where did he get the coffee?"

"He called room service for it."

"Does he often do that?"

Michael smiled. "Your questions are right on. I asked that myself. He said he frequently does, but not always."

"And does he remember who brought it?"

"He said it was a girl, but he didn't recognize her."

"Isn't room service usually delivered by boys?"

"Usually, but late at night. . . ." He shrugged. "Jim's checking it."

They talked throughout the meal and were just finishing their guava sherbet when the lights of the restaurant went out, leaving only the flickering of candles on white linen-covered tables. A brown-skinned Hawaiian youth wearing only a red malos tied around his waist strode across the bridge that spanned the lagoon just beyond Susan's and Michael's seats. When the boy reached the middle of the bridge he stood with feet planted firmly apart and blew a haunting call on the conch shell he was carrying. All was still in the coconut grove along the banks of Queen Liliuokalani's fish ponds on the ancient tribal grounds.

The conch sang a plaintive melody and a drum beat answered from beneath the trees. The soft voice of an aged islander began the tale of times long past in the islands when the tribal chieftains met on this very spot for council and ceremony. Susan felt as if she herself were a small child sitting around a fire being given the tradition of her people by the great grandmother of the race. In her mind she could see the flames flickering on the venerable, wrinkled, brown face of the story-teller and the light reflected in the rapt eyes of the children sitting around her in a circle, intent on every word.

And then the drum beat built to a crescendo and through the ancient palm grove a malos-clad young man came running, his torch flaming streamers behind him. As he ran he swung the torch in great rhythmic circles and each time it reached the bottom of the circle a torch pot burst into fire. Back and forth he ran, touching his flame to scores of torches until the entire grove was ablaze with the light of flaring, flickering torchlight. And then the sound of the conch died on the trembling air and the runner stepped into an outrigger canoe. With his torch still flaring, he glided away into the darkness, leaving the enchanted watchers to wonder if he had ever really been there at all, or if they had seen the ghost of a runner that had performed this ancient tribal rite hundreds of years ago.

When they arrived back at the Langford, Susan was still in the magic spell woven by the conch player, the storyteller, and the torch runner. Michael seemed to sense her mood as he directed her steps, not toward the hotel lobby, but to the beach. Susan took off her delicate strappy sandals and Michael put them in his pocket. Hand-in-hand they walked out onto the beach. A gentle sea breeze wafted the light fabric of her full-skirted dress and tugged playfully at the tendrils of her hair. Michael's eyes shone as he looked at her.

The sand still held the warmth of the sun and Susan's stocking-clad toes wiggled in the soft grains. "Don't you wish you could have seen it all a hundred years ago when Queen Liliuokalani was reigning and the natives worked and played on the beaches unhindered by tourists and condominium developments?" she said with a sigh.

Michael laughed gently. "You'd have me believe you're a hardened cynic, but underneath it all you're really an incurable romantic, aren't you?"

"I'm neither. I'm a realist!" For some reason it seemed very important to her, that he should understand this about her. "If I try something and it doesn't work, I discard it. That's not cynical or romantic—that's common sense."

"And since you don't want to make the same mistake twice, nothing and no one gets a second chance?"

She was quiet, not sure how to answer him. She felt

as if she were a hostile witness having her deposition taken.

"I remember that lawyers were one of the things you'd discarded. I was hoping you'd decided to give us another chance—at least some of us."

Relieved that that was the only one of her biases he was leading up to, she relaxed a little. "Well, it seems that I am, doesn't it?"

And then, as she knew he would, and had been longing for him to, he took her in his arms and held her tight against him. He kissed her neck, making her thrill clear down to the sand. It was like the igniting of the torches. The world spun deliciously. Tilted. Then righted itself.

They stood for some time looking out toward the bay. A sprinkling of stars was shining in the dark sky and just a tiny sliver of a moon made a silver arc above them. Michael kept one arm securely around Susan and held her tightly to him.

At last the pounding of her heart subsided to below the level of the beating waves. "Let's walk a bit," she said and pulled slightly ahead of him to move down the beach. Each lost in thought, they walked wordlessly for some time with Susan in the lead.

Suddenly she gave a small cry. "Oh, that's cold!" Intending to walk parallel to the water, she had mindlessly walked into the foamy tide.

"You know, I really worry about you," Michael said, drawing her back up on the dry sand. "Don't you ever watch where you're going?"

He was always so calm—so self-possessed. "Don't *you* ever get rattled? Doesn't anything *ever* overwhelm you?"

He was quiet for a moment. Even in the dim light she could see his gray eyes looking at her. "It's called living by faith." The words were spoken as softly as a prayer.

She recoiled as if he'd slapped her. In the joy of his company, in the rapture of his embrace, she had forgotten the gulf that separated them. The phrase was trite but they really did live in two different worlds.

"I want to go in now," she said sadly.

CHAPTER 7

THE NEXT MORNING SUSAN awoke to a definitely "blue Monday." Maybe Josh was right after all. Why *was* she putting herself through all this? She had organized the office; set up files on menus, tours, and meeting facilities; launched *Aloha*; streamlined security operations. Now why couldn't she train someone to take her place? After all, she'd only come here on temporary assignment to straighten things out and she'd pretty well done that. She'd talk to Ted about it today, she decided as she got out of bed.

She should have been exhilarated to have reached a decision, but the thought of returning to her old apartment, her old job, her old boyfriend, made her unspeakably depressed. She had glimpsed paradise and nothing less would satisfy her.

She washed her face, scrubbing her delicate skin harder than she really meant to. As she brushed her hair and applied just a touch of make up she studied her reflection. She was shocked to meet a look of sunny sweetness in the mirror. Her inner cynicism and turmoil didn't show in her bright blue eyes or in the smile on her soft lips. She supposed that was something to be thankful for, but at the moment her mood was sufficiently perverse that she would have liked to inflict her feelings on others with a sour look.

She spent the morning with the house photographer taking pictures of elegant guests in exotic settings for *Aloha*. Back in her office, she opened the mail. Linda had sent her a copy of *Cable Car*, the house publicity organ for the Langford San Francisco, and Susan was happy to see how well she had trained her assistant there. The thought crossed her mind that perhaps they didn't really need her back at her old job. What if they didn't even want her? Of course it had been understood that she could come back when the mess in Kauai was dealt with, but she wondered how Linda would take it now that she'd had the experience of being in charge of everything?

Well, that was Linda's problem—Susan had enough of her own. Of course, if Linda quit or became surly, it would be Susan's problem, too. *Well*, Susan told herself, *You're not back yet. You can worry about that when the time comes.* She smiled as she thought that she was beginning to feel a kinship for Scarlet O'Hara and her, "I'll think about that tomorrow" philosophy. She picked up a stack of folders and turned to the file cabinet in the corner of the room.

"I thought I'd find you here. . . ." Michael's voice breaking in suddenly on her reverie startled Susan so that she spun around, bumping her elbow painfully on the edge of the file cabinet. "Did you stand me up intentionally, or did you forget what time it is?"

Susan gasped. She had promised to spend the afternoon with Michael. He said he had a surprise for her. Before she could answer him the phone on her desk rang.

She gave Michael a brief smile to acknowledge his

presence and picked up the receiver. It was Ted with orders for the evening. She was to check out a luau at the rival hotel. The Langford was considering initiating one and he wanted her to see what she thought of it.

When she told Michael he shook his head and laughed. "Well, now we know why your predecessor walked off the job. She had probably just received similar orders."

"What do you mean?" asked Susan. "I think it sounds like fun."

"The only person who thinks a luau sounds like fun is someone who hasn't been to one. Well, never mind, orders are orders. I'll see you through it."

"Well, *thank you*," she said sarcastically. "But I wouldn't dream of putting you out."

"Oh, no. You can't shake me off like that. *I* wouldn't consider letting you face it alone. Good thing we've got a nice afternoon ahead of us first. Got your suit?"

Susan told him she'd just be a minute and ran up to her room. It was a hot day, the temperature rising almost as fast as the humidity. Michael was wearing shorts, so Susan chose a pair of shorts and a sun top to pull on over her suit.

They were soon driving along a narrow winding road that took them through sugar cane plantations and jungle verdancy. They drove past a Catholic cemetery filled with statues of the saints and a tall graceful Madonna at the focal point; then around the next curve, a Buddhist cemetery with a huge white stone Buddha sitting in the midst of the graves of his believers.

The road wound up a steep incline, getting narrower and narrower. At last it just ended.

"How strange! Why would anyone build a road that just ends nowhere?" Susan asked.

Michael shrugged. "Who knows? Maybe they ran out of money. Maybe they just got tired. Maybe they figured this was close enough." He took her hand and helped her from the car.

"Close enough to what?"

"Come on. I'll show you." He took a basket from the back seat and then locked the car. When they had hiked a few thousand feet along a dirt trail, Susan's ear caught the tumultuous roar of falling water.

"Oh, a waterfall," she cried, hurrying along the path.

Then she stopped. She stood looking with wonder into the canyon just below her feet. The crevice ended in a box a short distance away and at the end a waterfall coursed like a bridal veil over black rocks and disappeared beneath the trees that filled the gorge. Even from this distance the power and energy of the cascade communicated its potent force.

"Look," Michael said, pointing to the sky. Like giant prehistoric birds, two hang gliders soared in the blue sky above them. Susan watched breathlessly as the red and yellow wings swooped and soared, riding the air currents.

"Daedalus and Icarus revisited," Michael said, his face tilted to the sky, watching the flyers.

"That must be the most incredible sense of free-dom—to actually be able to fly with the birds," Susan mused. The freedom of the gliders and the force of the waterfall made sharp contrast in her mind to the confining void of the little cemeteries they had passed. It all made life seem so achingly short. Much too short to waste even one day in worry and frustration. Her job . . . Josh . . . Michael . . . it would all work out. In college they had been fond of saying that "God had a plan for everything." She certainly refused to believe that—but it would work out anyway. Somehow.

Michael held out his free hand and she took it. Her

104

hand was small and delicately white inside his strong bronzed fingers.

"Come on," he said. "I know a trail that's not for convention-goers."

The way into the gorge was steep and rocky, but Michael held her hand securely. She often grasped the branches of small bushes growing along the path for an extra handhold, but she never slipped. At the bottom the roar of the water was louder and was accompanied by babbling sounds from the small river running through the canyon away from the falls.

The vegetation was much thicker here than it had been up on top of the ravine. There were tall bushy trees and verdant underbrush, giving a sense of privacy as if they were alone in a primeval creation.

"Look!" Susan said with surprise and delight. "A pineapple growing on a tree! I didn't know they did that!"

Michael laughed gently and kissed her forehead. "What a delightful *makaikai* you are. That is a tourist pineapple. I think God created it as a practical joke on newcomers."

"Well, it certainly *looks* like a pineapple," she said defensively. "But what did you call me?"

"*Makaikai*—visitor or newcomer," he replied, still smiling.

"Is it good for anything but making people feel like fools? Seems like your God should have had something better than that to do with his time."

Michael was still smiling as he led her slowly in the direction of the waterfall. "Well, the fruit is sweet, but it's usually only eaten in hard times. The leaves are used for weaving: baskets, hats, slippers, screens, rugs, mats—"

"Okay, okay, you've made your point," she said good-naturedly.

And then another jungle plant caught her eye.

"Orchids!" she cried. "I heard they grew wild here, but I've never seen them before."

The exotic plants produced sprays of blossoms along long stems, growing in the shade at the base of trees, tucked in banks of ferns. They came in all shades: pale lavender with deep orchid throats, tiny yellow blossoms with ruffled edges, rusty mauve flowers growing on yellow stems, green-tinged white with rust spotted throats, deep purple so dark it was almost black, delicate white and lavender striped.

The familiar vanda orchids, which served as garnish on so many dinner plates, grew in sprays of as many as eight to a branch and were the only variety she knew by name. They were all small, not the hybrid hot house varieties worn by mothers-of-the-bride, although she had seen some of those growing in cultivated gardens.

"It really is Eden," she said, shaking her head in wonder.

They suddenly broke through the thick covering of plants into an open area and stood on the edge of a narrow white sandbar running around a deep green pool in an almost perfect circle. Susan stood with Michael's arm around her looking at the powerful, frothy cascade plunging into the depths of the jade pool at her feet until she was mesmerized by its hypnotic effect. Sunlight caught droplets of the mist in the air and produced a bright rainbow that completely arched the pool.

The tumult of the falling water engulfed their senses, and yet the roar seemed to be strangely quieter than it was farther down the canyon. "That's strange," remarked Susan. "I thought we'd be deafened here."

"Something to do with the way the canyon walls reflect the sound. I'm afraid I don't really know enough about acoustics to understand it fully."

"Well, I finally found *something* you don't know!" Susan gloated.

They pulled off their shorts and shirts and swam in the seafoam pool, cavorting and splashing each other like water sprites. The icy water was a shock to Susan when she first took the plunge into its depths, but with the hot sun warming the air around them it was soon delectable.

Susan floated on her back, rocked by the motion of the water, and looked at the wall of white water at the other end of the pool, at the luxuriant green softness covering the canyon walls, and at the blue ceiling overhead. The water washed her body with its fresh cleanness and the sun kissed her face with a promise of joy.

She turned her head slightly to see Michael beside her. He swam a few strokes closer to shore where he could touch bottom and then reached out to her.

Being kissed in a waterfall pool was a new experience to Susan. But every time Michael kissed her it was a new experience. His kiss held the power and vibrancy of the waterfall and it sent her soaring even higher than the hang gliders flew. She was more completely his than ever before. She couldn't touch ground here, and as he held her against him, the water wrapped them in a satiny closeness. Susan responded with all the warmth and tenderness of her nature. Even as it was happening, Susan knew this was a moment that came once in a lifetime and ever afterwards life would be different because of the sweet intensity of this memory.

He kissed her again and again on the lips, her cheeks, her eyes, her neck, and she kissed him back. At last with an ache so strong they could almost hear the tearing sound, they pulled apart. But not far apart. Their arms still around each other, they moved up to the white circle of the beach.

The sand was hot under their feet. For the first time Susan noticed the clear sound of birdsong in the trees all around them. Still holding her tightly, Michael led her along the silvery sand right up to the waterfall and then a little ways into the undergrowth to the left.

"My brother and I discovered this. It was our favorite spot and our greatest secret," he said, curving back toward the falls and leading her into a narrow ledge that went behind the veil of white water. He had to lean down and speak right into her ear because here the full roar of the water was audible with no acoustical tricks to muffle it. And yet the noise was part of the enchantment of the spot. Not only were they hidden from sight but also from the sound of the world in their secret damp grotto. There was not an enormous quantity of water rushing over the mountain and into the pool, but it fell from such great height that its effect was magnified. The sun shining on the crystalline fall made it almost transparent and they could see the green world beyond as through a window washed by bright rain. But there was no glass wall to keep the spray off them. Susan gave an involuntary shiver.

"It is cold in here. Let's go back," Michael said in her ear.

She nodded.

Back on the beach Michael brought out the basket he had carried down and spread a glorious repast before them. Susan groaned with delight as she hungrily eyed the thick slices of roast chicken, slabs of homemade brown bread and butter, deviled eggs, tangy pickles, bright red strawberries, and tiny almond cookies.

"Your catering department is very efficient," Michael said, offering her a glass of lemonade from the thermos he had just opened.

They ate ravenously and laughed at their own

greediness. Then Susan stretched out languidly on the towel which had also been tucked in the basket. Michael left her for a moment and returned with an orchid spray, which he entwined in her hair. To her amazement he also produced a bottle of sun tan lotion.

"You do think of everything, don't you?"

He grinned. "I thought you might not remember it." And then his hands were caressing her as he applied the smooth cream to her satiny skin.

She was floating on a lovely pink cloud when suddenly she sat up. "Oh, no. What time is it? I'd forgotten about the luau."

Michael picked up his shorts and took his watch out of a pocket. "You're right. We'll have to hurry."

Susan was so excited as she got ready for the luau that she even sang the few strains she knew of the beautiful "Aloha Oe." She was sure Michael had exaggerated about the horrors of a hotel luau. She knew some people just didn't like unusual foods. Maybe that was what he meant. It seemed to be a tradition for tourists to turn up their noses at poi, but she was determined to like it.

Susan's head was full of visions of sitting on mats on a beach beneath tall palm trees, eating succulent roast pork while the moon shone on them overhead and the soft strains of island music floated to them on air that also bore the scent of tropical flowers. Now what could possibly go wrong with that?

She even had a special outfit she'd been saving for just such an occasion. It was a red, orange, and pink handkerchief print skirt with a hemline that hung to her ankles in sharp v's at front, back, and sides, and rose to her knees between. The red halter-back, wrap-around top in a soft knit fabric made her feel very sophisticated and very sexy at the same time. She carried a lightweight knit shawl to throw over her bare shoulders in case it got cool on the beach later. She even splashed on generous dabs of frangipani perfume in the best local tradition.

Susan was surprised to see it was ten minutes past the hour when she was ready; Michael was never late. She paced the floor restlessly; she didn't want to miss the beginning of the festivities. Another turn around the room and she looked at her clock. Three minutes had passed. What on earth was keeping him?

When Michael's knock finally came she hurried out the door to meet him. A sharp gust of wind blowing through the corridor made her forget about the lateness of the hour in a more immediate concern, "Oh, no! They won't have to cancel the luau will they?" she cried, eyeing the threatening clouds the brisk breeze was blowing in.

"Not on your life. At twenty-some dollars a ticket the hotel won't cancel a luau for anything less than a full-scale hurricane."

"Now who's being the cynic?" she returned with a smile.

Michael might be cynical about luaus but he looked smashing, she thought as she surveyed with pleasure his trim-fitting white slacks and white island shirt decorated, not in the loud floral prints of most local wear, but with white-on-white stitchery. Even his open-weave white shoes looked as if they had been made especially for the occasion.

On their way to the car they passed a bush of bright red hibiscus bending in the wind. Susan picked a blossom and pinned it in her hair where she had already swept it up and back with a pearl comb.

Susan's first fantasy was shattered when they arrived at the hotel and Michael led her, not to the beach, as she had envisioned, but to a sturdily covered patio behind the hotel. "But I thought it would be on the beach," she objected. "The advertisements said this was Kauai's most authentic luau. Surely the ancients didn't have their luaus on covered patios!"

"At least this way we'll be protected if it decides to rain," Michael said, looking at the dark clouds gathering overhead.

As the long line they were waiting in to enter the luau area inched ahead (also not included in Susan's daydream was standing in line), the wind whipped at the plastic awnings pulled down around the dining area. The wind also tugged at Susan's skirt and hair, and she had to admit she would be grateful for the protection, even if it wasn't authentic.

"I meant to apologize for being late," Michael said, "but judging from this line maybe I should have been later."

"Thank you. You're too gallant."

"No, I didn't mean I should have kept you waiting longer," he said with the boyish grin that never failed to produce a flip-flop feeling in her. "I was tied up on the phone. Heather was having some problems she really needed to talk through. I suppose it's good for the ego to be made to feel indispensable, but the timing was bad."

Susan's stomach lurched. "Heather who?"

But as Susan voiced her question the music began. Not the gentle strains of steel guitars or of ancient island instruments that Susan had heard in her vision, but a very loud guitar and vocalist performing country and western music. Susan looked at Michael, and he shook his head with a grin. *Well, at least he didn't say "I told you so,"* she thought.

At the door Susan was greeted by a handsome, if sweaty, Hawaiian man who put a shell lei around her neck, kissed her, and wished her "Aloha." She didn't look, but she knew Michael was receiving a similar treatment from the mumu-clad girl on the other side. But Susan's mind was still on Michael's earlier remark. Who was this Heather whose name kept cropping up? And why was Michael "indispensable" to her? Had he edited his account of old flames, just as Susan had?

Before taking their seats on the folding metal chairs at the long white tables (a far cry from Susan's romanticized mats under palm trees) they passed the bar where they were offered the traditional Mai Tai rum and fruit drinks. Michael smiled and asked for pineapple juice, but Susan defiantly accepted hers. He may be indispensable to Heather, but she'd show him he wasn't to Susan.

Michael held a chair for her near the end of one of the long tables and chose to sit beside her, rather than across the table. The line was still snaking in, and food had not yet been set out on the serving tables. It looked like a long evening. But the master of ceremonies on the stage was determined not to let a moment drag. When he wasn't accosting them with loud music he used the time to tell crowd-warmer jokes that Susan never seemed to get the point of, or if she did, wished she hadn't.

Her Mai Tai was long gone when the host, after receiving uproarious cheers for his special welcome to a convention of farm implement dealers from the midwest, urged everyone back for more drinks, "On the house, all you want." The wind whipped the awnings and blew a blast of cold air through the room. Susan tied her shawl around her shoulders and decided she needed another drink.

Michael quietly brought her drink and a refill on his canned pineapple juice. His refusal to show what she was certain must be disapproval of her behavior made Susan feel even more rebellious. Why didn't he say something so she could argue with him? Who did he think he was to be so accepting?

The entertainers initiated a sing-along time and all around them the partiers were singing loudly and clapping their hands. Since conversation with Michael was impossible in that din, Susan tried to read her menu describing the tradition of the luau: "The original meaning of the Hawaiian word *luau* is 'young taro tops,' the most important crop cultivated for local consumption. But beginning in the year 1856 the word came to mean a Hawaiian feast. The change came when a young newspaper reporter wrote a story about a luau he attended. Because there were so many taro, or luau, dishes at the feast, he thought the whole party was called a luau."

So I suppose we have him to thank for this, Susan thought wryly, as the noise in the room threatened to overwhelm her. She took a sip of her drink and staunchly read on, "The basic fare of a luau is a pig cooked in an *imu*, an underground oven formed by heated rocks. The pig, wrapped first in banana leaves, then in wet ti leaves, takes on a delicious smoked flavor and becomes moist and tender. The final product is called *Kalua pig*." *Well*, she thought, *at least the food will be good*.

She had begun to think it would never happen, but at last it was announced that the food was ready and guests could help themselves at the buffet tables. Susan was starving and since they were at the back of the room, they were among the first in line. The food was presented beautifully, each dish being labeled and garnished with flowers, and leaves with branches of flowers were strewn on the tables between the serving dishes. It made a sumptuous setting for the food of Old Hawaii. Things were looking up, Susan thought.

The colorful *Lomi Salmon* appealed to Susan so she took a generous portion of the chilled, salted, shredded salmon mixed with tomatoes and green onions. She had read on her menu that *Lomilomi* means to

113

massage and this process makes the fish deliciously tender and juicy. She avoided the jello and potato salads, but helped herself to Chicken Long Rice, an oriental dish that was long ago adopted for luaus. Long rice, Susan saw to her surprise, was like slippery, clear spaghetti.

Since this was a traditional "old fashioned" luau, the menu also included: squid, chilled and sliced into round white dollars; raw fish marinated in a hot sauce with chopped seaweed; and *Kalo,* taro cooked in the imu. And of course Susan took one of the little dishes of poi, although she was just a bit disconcerted to see that it was purple. Somewhere she had heard the comment that it tasted like wallpaper paste, so she had assumed it would be white. The large platters of assorted fresh fruits were beautiful and she filled the few empty spots on her plate with a colorful selection. There was no breadfruit; it was out of season. Another image destroyed.

They had no more than resumed their seats and begun to eat than the entertainers returned from their break and again regaled the jocular crowd with music. Next on the agenda was ascertaining where everyone was from by naming a state and seeing which one received the most deafening shouts. When California was called Susan took a bite of Kalua pig and was almost choked by its heavy, greasy flavor. She washed it down with a swallow of Mai Tai.

She decided to try the *lauai pea me ka ohi'a*—avocado and tomato salad with mushrooms and cucumbers. At least that was a success, as was the crab salad. She wondered how authentically ancient some of the ingredients were, but the flavor was excellent.

A waiter passed by with a tray of Mai Tais and Susan took another. Michael leaned close to her ear, "Would you like me to get you a glass of authentic canned pineapple juice?"

The room was warming up and Susan threw her shawl back from her shoulders. The music was beginning to sound better, too. This wasn't such a bad party after all. Michael just wasn't into the spirit of things. That was the trouble with being a fanatic— you couldn't have any fun. "No thank you," she replied with dignity. "These are deelishus." And she took a big drink.

For just an instant there was a look on his face that reminded her of Phillip, whom she had once thought she loved long ago. A look of . . . could it be compassion? What a repugnant thought. But even as she mutinously took a swallow of her drink, it flashed through her mind to wonder if she had been happier then? Not with Phillip, of course, but with—her mind boggled at the possibilities for filling in that blank: Faith? Belief? God?

She took another drink. "Deelishus," she repeated.

Unfortunately, she couldn't say the same for any of the rest of the food on her plate. The squid tasted like rubbery lard, the baked taro was unspeakable, and she wouldn't have liked the raw fish even if she hadn't known it was raw fish. In traditional style she dipped her fingers in the poi and licked it off, telling herself she was going to love it. She hated it. Melted plastic couldn't possibly have been as bad as that. Only a stiff drink of her cocktail enabled her to get the gluey substance down, rather than spit it out.

That left a small white square of *haupia*, a coconut milk pudding that, after being boiled, takes on the texture of gelatin. It wasn't great; but it was edible.

The lights dimmed, the convention revellers quieted, and the Polynesian Extravaganza program began. The incessant, restless rhythm of jungle drums beat in the background, and Susan and Michael turned their chairs to face the stage for a better view. A brown-skinned young man ran the length of the room, holding a flaming torch aloft. To the strains of "The Hawaiian War Chant" he did a thrilling Samoan fire dance exhibition. He transferred the flame from one end of the torch to the other by holding a bit of flame in his bare hand, then with his torch flaming at both ends, he leaped and gyrated, throwing the torch high into the air and sometimes catching it with his teeth. He lighted another torch and spun them both in intricate flaming patterns, giving the impression of a fireworks display. When he lay on his back and rotated the burning sticks with his bare feet Susan broke into enthusiastic applause with the rest of the audience.

Next on the program was a group of four Polynesian girls wearing grass skirts made from freshly picked ti leaves. Their grass skirts rustled, their red leis swung rhythmically, and their waist-length black hair swayed gracefully as their hips and arms undulated in the storytelling motions of a hula dance. Then the girls played some old folk instruments, including calabash gourds, feathered shakers, and long sticks to accompany a pretty young girl in a long pink tropical dress in her solo dances. Susan swayed in her chair in time with the music. She was sure she could do those dances too, even though island girls begin their hula training when they are four or five years old.

To give the dancing girls time to change costumes, the host took the stage and after learning, by the means of much shouting and arm-waving, which couples in the audience were having an anniversary that month, he sang "The Hawaiian Wedding Song" to them. The room was spinning a bit, but Susan thought the song was beautiful. One couple volunteered that they had been married fifty-two years. She wondered if she'd ever be married fifty-two years. It seemed impossible. "This room is hot," she complained thickly.

The dancers re-entered for a spectacular Tahitian dance number. They wore floor-length grass skirts of a natural straw color, adorned with heavy red tassels and fringes. Their headpieces stood more than two feet high, with hats that looked like inverted baskets and floral streamers arched high overhead and flowing down their backs. They carried straw pompoms which they waved seductively at the men in the front rows.

"And now the moment you've all been waiting for, Ladies and Gentlemen. It's time for our traditional Hula contest—starring *You*! Now I know you'll all want to take part in the fun. Come on, let's all get into the spirit! Everybody on your feet now. Our lovely hula girls will come around and give you individualized lessons before we pick our winners. Now remember, it's all done with the hands—the hands tell the story."

The music began but was quickly muffled by the scraping of chairs on the cement floor, shuffling feet, and laughing people. "Come on, Mike, let's show 'em how to do it," Susan said as she swayed on her feet.

Even in her unsteady condition she was aware of the glare in his steely gray eyes. "Don't be a spoilsport," she said. "Loosen up and live a little!" She gave a strident laugh; Michael did not smile.

One of the dancing girls approached them. "Would the lady like to come up on stage for our contest?" she asked.

"Sure I would. Come with me, Mike."

"The lady is going home," he said quickly but firmly.

Susan turned in a fury. "What do you mean? I'm having a good time! Don't be such a sanctimonious stick-in-the-mud!"

The dancers moved on to other guests.

"You just think you're better than the rest of us because you've got some kind of a hotline to

117

Heaven!" She flung the words out. Right now she'd like to kick him and hit him and scratch him with her fingernails—anything to break through his composure.

He picked up her stole, grasped her firmly by both arms, and marched her ahead of him toward the door. "Excuse us," he said curtly, as partiers moved back to clear a path for them.

"Where do you think you're taking me? I want to win that contest!" she insisted as they exited.

A blast of cold wind with rain behind it made her catch her breath. She sagged heavily against Michael and allowed him to lead her to the car. By the time they were back at the hotel she was sobbing. Her thoughts were running along the line of "Michael's no fun and he doesn't want me to have any fun. I hate him and he hates me." She didn't have any idea how much of it all she said aloud.

Michael took her in the back way and up the elevator to avoid having to walk through the front lobby. At her door he grasped her shoulders firmly and spun her around to him. "Now listen to me, Susan," he said firmly. "You are to go in there and undress and go to bed. Can you manage that or shall I call a maid?"

Susan summoned all her decorum and said as steadily as she could, "Of course I can. I do that every night. What do you think?"

Michael opened the door, then locked it again before closing it behind her. Leaning on the dresser for support and blinking to clear her focus, Susan looked at herself in the mirror. On top of everything else the hibiscus blossom in her hair had wilted.

CHAPTER 8

THE RINGING OF THE PHONE WAS a shattering experience for Susan the next morning. Her head felt as big as the whole room and it was not only as if the phone were ringing inside her head—clanging on the raw nerves there—but also flinging itself around from one side of her brain to the other, bruising every spot it touched.

She lifted the receiver gingerly. She didn't want to talk to anyone. She couldn't do it. She set the receiver beside the phone, pulled a pillow over her head and floated in black misery.

The next thing she knew it was not a telephone leaping about in her head, but a sledge hammer, making sharp pounding noises and leaving bleeding wounds wherever it hit. When all attempts to shut out the noise failed, Susan gradually became aware that someone was knocking on her door. She pulled another pillow over her head and groaned loudly. Maybe they would think she had died and go away. With a little luck maybe she *would* die.

The knocking did not stop, so finally, holding her head with both hands, and walking very carefully, Susan groped her way to the door. Just turning the lock required the most phenomenal effort of concentration.

"Please be quiet. You'll disturb the other guests," she commanded in a raspy whisper.

Through the open slit in the door Michael's gray eyes glinted in amusement. "I thought you might be feeling like this," he said. "I brought you something to help." He held out a tall glass of ice and sparkling soda water.

"Just a minute," Susan muttered. She pulled on her robe, then undid the chain lock.

"No sermons," she instructed as she took the glass and settled on her bed.

"I wouldn't think of it. If virtue is its own reward, surely indulgence is its own punishment."

Holding her head with one hand, Susan put the glass of soda water to her lips with the other. She observed Michael, lean and relaxed in the black leather chair. She had never hated his virtue more than she did at that moment, comparing his vibrant well-being to her own condition and knowing that she had only herself to blame. And what must he think of her now? She had been searching desperately to find a way to handle their relationship, but making him despise her by her rebellious overindulgence wasn't exactly what she had in mind as a solution.

"I'm surprised you're speaking to me after last night."

"I'm here on business," he said curtly. "Mrs. Irving's insurance company has sent an investigator over. He's very suspicious. Seems this is the second set of jewelry she has filed a claim on."

"Mrs. Irving?" Susan asked dully, chewing on a piece of ice. The soda was beginning to settle her stomach. That was something at least.

"Mrs. Irving, the lady whose jewels were stolen from the hotel safe—you *do* remember about the robbery, don't you?"

She sighed and nodded. Then wished she hadn't, as the abrupt motion made her head swim again. She sank back against the headboard.

"Anyway, Aaron Strickland, that's the insurance investigator, would like to talk to you since you were the one who found Kele."

She groaned and closed her eyes. Only to help Lani and Kele would she make such a monumental effort.

One shower, two aspirin, and three glasses of water later, Susan sat in Ted Rawling's office being interviewed by the insurance man. "I've already told you twice about finding Kele on the beach. If I tell you six more times it won't change because I told you the way it was," she said testily.

"Now, Miss Jamison, I'm not suggesting you're lying. I'm just hoping there might be some detail you've forgotten—something that will help us," Aaron Strickland had thick black hair that was beginning to thin on top and to gray at the temples. He wore horn-rimmed glasses and a gray business suit with a long-sleeved white shirt and a necktie. He looked distinctly uncomfortable in the tropical climate.

"Since I've told you all I know, why don't you tell me what you know? Maybe that will suggest something to me." Susan doubted that it would, but listening was easier than talking.

"That's just the problem. We don't know very much, I'm afraid. Mrs. Irving checked the jewels into the hotel safe when she arrived. At the end of her two weeks' vacation she asked for them back and they were gone. Apparently they were taken that night because the money the day clerk deposited before going off duty that evening was gone too."

"If she never wore them, why did she bring them?" Susan asked.

"She claims she was afraid to leave them home because her antebellum house was to be included in a tour of stately Georgian mansions for some charity function while she was away."

"So why didn't she put them in a safety deposit box in her bank at home?"

"You are sharp, aren't you, Miss Jamison? We asked the same questions. She said she thought she might want them. She hadn't realized the islands were quite so casual."

Susan nodded. It had been a surprise for her, too. The atmosphere was decidedly laid back compared to the San Francisco lifestyle she had been used to. But she was finding that once you adjusted to it, it could be delightful.

"Michael said you were suspicious because this was her second claim?"

"Yes. In less than two years, as a matter of fact. Perhaps you read about the heist at an Atlanta United Fund ball? Several society matrons lost their family jewels, our Mrs. Irving among them. The suspicious part is that hers were the only ones not recovered."

"No wonder she was nervous about leaving them this time. Did they ever catch the thief?"

"No, but the case isn't closed yet."

"Well, I'm sorry I couldn't be of more help. I really must be getting to work now."

"Of course, Miss Jamison. Thank you for your time. And be sure to call me if you think of anything—even if it seems unimportant to you."

But back in her office, Susan found it impossible to accomplish anything. Her window was wide open in hopes of letting in any breezes that should decide to blow, but the room was oppressive. Last night's rain had served only to raise the humidity, not to freshen things. She sat at her desk staring blankly at the piles of paper and unopened mail there. The information Aaron Strickland had given her kept going around and around in her aching head. She wished she could help. She wondered why she had the vague feeling that something that was said should have rung a bell with her. It was like hearing just a snatch of a song that you knew you should be able to identify. Probably not important, but maddeningly frustrating.

She picked up her letter opener and slit open four letters. She read the first one through three times before she realized it was hopeless. She might as well give up and go for a swim. Maybe that would clear her head. At least it would cool her off. Her cotton knit dress was sticking to her and her hands felt clammy.

A few minutes later she fully appreciated what a good decision she had made. Nothing could possibly have revived her like this fresh, sparkling water. She even swam right under the man-made waterfall shielding the snack bar. The water droplets felt like prickling, sharp rain drops on her skin. And like prickling, sharp memory goads, they brought clearly before her mind the hours spent yesterday at the waterfall pool. She allowed herself to experience again the timeless glory of Michael's kiss . . . But then with chagrin, her mind went on to the evening. How could Michael possibly care for her after that? Surely she had killed any tender feelings he might be harboring. And yet he was so thoughtful this morning, bringing her a soda and no sermons.

How could he possibly care for her when she was so unworthy? She had done nothing to merit his kindness . . . with a rude interruption of her thoughts her head bumped into something soft and squishy. She was almost swamped by the churning water being thrashed by a child's arms and legs. When she regained her equilibrium Susan discovered she had floated into a little boy on an inflated polka dotted sea horse. The child thought it was great sport and was shrieking with delight as he continued to make war on the invader by splashing water at her.

"Wait! Stop! I'm sorry!" she cried, raising her hands in self defense.

"Arnie! You stop that splashing!" a lady commanded from the side of the pool. Arnie got in three more good splashes at the retreating Susan and then stopped.

Susan wrapped a towel around her wet hair and relaxed in a lounge chair to dry off in the sun. She would put in extra hours tomorrow to make up for her truancy today, she told herself. She closed her eyes and lay back in the chair, smiling to herself with a reminder she was going to have to be more careful in the future. This was the second collision she'd had in the pool in three days.

Her eyes flew open and she sat bolt upright. *That* was the baffling memory she couldn't get ahold of! Mrs. Irving was from Georgia. The girl she had bumped into in the pool was from Georgia. And didn't that girl—what *was* her name?—say she'd only been here about three weeks? That would just about coincide with Mrs. Irving's arrival time. Susan's mind raced. Just what if that girl had been the one who had delivered Kele's coffee! She said she worked for catering—that was right next to room service in a row of desks by the kitchen. . . .just maybe . . .

She grabbed her beach cover and ran for her room phone. Michael wasn't in his room. Nor was Jim in his. Maybe Aaron would still be in Ted's office. The phone rang in her ears three times. Jim answered.

Susan was aware of a stab of disappointment. She wanted to give her great lead to Michael. But it was too good to keep, so she told Jim.

"That's great, Sue!" he responded warmly. "I'll

get right on it and check it out. Where would I find employee records?"

"Right there in Ted's office, but you'll probably have to get the key from him."

"Right. That's great! Thanks again, kid."

Susan hung up, shaking her head. Very few people called her Sue and no one ever called her "kid." She just had time to get ready for her appointment. A group of travel agents from Honolulu were to be given the super deluxe tour of the Langford Kauai, complete with a poolside tea party, to encourage them to book their clients into the Langford when they made up itineraries for out-island tours. Susan blew her hair dry and brushed it to a bouncy golden cloud, then slipped into her crisp red skirt and sleeveless white blouse.

There were only six agents—four women and two men—to be shown around and Susan was thankful that she was now well enough acquainted with the hotel facilities to be able to answer their questions readily. With a brief stab of embarrassment she recalled ushering Michael into the service closet on her first day.

It took a full two hours of walking to cover the Langford's meeting rooms, guests' suites and rooms, restaurants, recreation facilities, and grounds. Susan was as glad as her guests were when it was time to relax at an umbrella-covered table by the pool and enjoy a cup of tea with an assortment of tiny cucumber and asparagus sandwiches.

Susan was gratified that her tour had been a success. As the agents left they assured her they were most favorably impressed and would be delighted to book their clients into the Langford. These were agents from the most exclusive agencies in the islands and their clientele were the type the Langford was designed to cater to. Susan smiled to herself as she thought, *exclusive people like Mrs. Irving.*

She saw her guests off in the hotel limousines and was retracing her steps back to the lobby when she saw Michael striding toward her. Her heart leaped to see him so unexpectedly. He was so arrestingly handsome in his trim-fitting dark slacks and light blue open-collared shirt.

She held out both of her hands, and he took them in his. He gave her the briefest of kisses on her cheek. "Congratulations, Super-sleuth! Your lead was just what we needed to crack the case."

"Tell me about it!" she cried.

They sat in the overstuffed chairs in the lobby, surrounded by tall potted plants. "We're sure now that Kele was drugged by Anne Marie who was Mrs. Irving's former secretary and was on duty in catering that night," he told her.

"Did Anne Marie crack the safe?"

"We don't think so. It was probably the chauffeur. Jim's working on that angle now."

"How sure are you of all this?" Susan was so relieved and happy for her friends she was almost afraid to believe it was true.

"We're sure enough that the police have booked Anne Marie for questioning. She had apparently stayed behind to keep an eye on the investigation, in case anything went wrong."

"They took her in already?"

"Yes, Jim called in the police as soon as we had a strong lead—yours. They've sent an APB mainland for Mrs. Irving and the chauffeur."

"What about Kele?" She held her breath. Michael hadn't mentioned the most important part yet—she didn't really care what happened to some society matron running an insurance fraud. She wanted to know about her friends.

"All charges have been dropped and he starts back on duty tonight."

"Oh, that's wonderful!" Susan clasped her hands in a gesture of thankfulness and delight. "Where's Lani? I want to celebrate with her!"

"Too late. The last time I saw her she and Kele were taking off to celebrate together."

"Oh, of course. They must be delirious!" Suddenly she got very serious. "Michael, thank you so much." She lay a hand on his arm. "You're the one who took care of everything. This happy ending might have been a very different story if you hadn't been here." Her throat closed on her and her eyes were brimming. His combination of strength and kindness was overwhelming.

"Since you can't celebrate with Lani, would I do as a substitute? I did have something in mind for tonight."

"What is it?"

"It wouldn't be a surprise if I told you, would it? Go put on something warm that it won't hurt to get damp."

As she was changing into her white pantsuit and dusty pink sweater with a wide cowl neckline she found herself thinking of the same time yesterday when she had been so happily preparing for the luau. What a disaster! She still couldn't believe Michael would even speak to her after that fiasco. And yet the only reference to it had come from her.

As her mind ran over the evening she realized how far apart they really were. They could have fun sightseeing, they could share unbelievable kisses, but their fundamental lives were lived in totally different spheres. And neither of them was likely to change. She knew she couldn't. She'd tried it. She sighed as she slipped her feet into canvas shoes. Maybe it was a good thing it had happened. *Now we both know where we stand*, she thought. Since the blow had to come sooner or later, it might as well be sooner. It was inevitable.

Michael led her not to the parking lot, but out the back of the lobby to the beach. "Where are we going?" she asked.

He pointed with a smile to the broad blue and white striped sails of the hotel's catamaran waiting for them on the sand. "To see the sunset."

She was thrilled. She had read the brochures about the romantic sunset cruises around the harbor, but hadn't had time to explore them. Michael and the captain helped her aboard and settled her comfortably with cushions on the wooden benches in the middle of the boat.

The captain, a tall, curly-haired, darkly tanned man, introduced himself as Billy and explained he would be serving as both captain and crew for the cruise.

"I've never been on a catamaran before," replied Susan. "Tell me about it. What makes them so special?"

"A monohull—like a regular sailboat—sails at a constant heel," he tipped his hand sideways to indicate a list. "The two pontoons of the catamaran are more stable."

His explanation was delivered with pride and Susan could see she had asked the right question if she wished to engage Billy in conversation. "Good, then that means it would be less likely to have an accident?" she asked.

Billy's face fell ever so slightly, "Well, there is very little of the boat below the water—like a raft—that can make it a little top heavy at times. But," he hurried on, "that means less water resistance and allows a catamaran to skim the water twice as fast as a monohull. You'll like it," he finished with a smiling flash of white teeth.

"I'm sure I will," agreed Susan. "Are these just tourists attractions, or something the ancients used?"

"Mostly just tourists now," Billy said with a nod. "The man who developed them more than sixty years ago still lives on Oahu—an eighty-year-old beach bum. But they are a native concept used long ago for fishing and traveling between islands.

Susan smiled her thanks at her informant and settled back in the cushions next to Michael. She was surprised when Billy began pushing the boat away from the beach. "Where are the others? I didn't think they went out with fewer than six couples," she said to Michael.

"I, ah, persuaded them." The humor in his eyes danced at her, like the last ray of sun on the silver water.

"You mean you bought *all* the tickets!" she gasped. "Why that must have cost . . ." She faltered, unable to do the figures in her head.

"It was a bargain. I wanted to share this sunset alone with you."

She knew she should have simply said thank you and melted against the arm that was around her shoulder, but her earlier thoughts were still with her like sharp goads. "But I thought Christians were supposed to be so frugal—stewardship or something," she said. Apparently he hadn't grasped the object lesson that last night had provided.

"Susan," he took his arm from her shoulders, turned to face her, and gripped her hands tightly. Now his eyes weren't twinkling like silver waves, they looked deep into her with a level intensity like smoky coals. "When will you start thinking of me as a person? As a man? And not as a stereotype of some poor misguided person you once knew?"

"What do you mean?" she asked softly, avoiding his gaze. She was afraid to ask. She most certainly thought of him as a man—the most virile, most magnetic man she had ever met. His attachment to an outmoded religion that she had abandoned years ago was her only shield against him.

"You told me you grew up with it, so you should know that Christianity is the most freeing force on earth. It frees people from fear, from guilt, from sin. And its freedom is free. If you've known some long-faced types who were trying to earn their salvation and laboring under an impossible burden then I'm very very sorry for them. But you must realize they've got it all wrong. God offers it all as an absolutely free gift—trying to earn His grace will just put you further from it."

She was trembling. He put his arm around her and drew her head down on his shoulder. "End of sermon. Now try to relax and enjoy the sunset we came out to see. This is my last night here, Susan. Let's not spoil it with our differences."

Susan had started to sink back against the seat, but she sat up quickly. "What? I thought you were staying the rest of the week."

"When I checked in with the office this afternoon I got some bad news. Remember the property I told you about recovering for that widow?"

Susan nodded, "That long, long case that you finally won."

"That's it. Well, the other side has filed an appeal."

"But can they do that?"

"I don't think they have the grounds, but that's why I have to get right back—to study the issues and see what I can do to protect my client. She's not in very good health and besides needing the income from that property now, I'm not sure she's physically able to stand up to a lengthy appeal."

"Oh." It was a depressed little sound, all she was capable of at the moment. Well, she had wanted him to prove that a lawyer could be upright and caring. So now he'd done it, now that she didn't really need proof anyway. *And I suppose Heather needs you, too?* Her mind screamed it, but her voice refused to repeat it.

The boat sailed due east out of Nawiliwili Harbor. Billy adjusted the sails, which he explained were jib forward and mainsail back, and the catamaran began tacking parallel to the island in the open sea. Susan, intent on blinking back her disappointment and suspicion, hadn't been paying attention to the scenery. Now, as Michael squeezed her shoulder and pointed, she raised her eyes with a cry of delight.

They were sailing in a world of color. The sun, sinking behind the island, shed a rim of molten gold on the horizon. The sky above reflected a dazzling array of chromatics flamboyantly emblazoned on the clouds. The orange, apricot, and flame-colored hues above the horizons shaded into a whole spectrum of purples, violets, and magentas. The iridescent display continued on up over their heads until it was as if they were inside a colossal parti-colored silk tent.

And the water around them was a sea of fire as it echoed the exhibition, adding a vibrancy of its own. Lights that were orange in the sky danced in scarlet and crimson swells on the ripples of the surface. Tongues of cerise and maroon lapped around them and droplets of water fell like handfuls of rubies, amethysts, and topazes flung into the spangled seascape.

Neither Susan nor Michael spoke. They were caught and held in this world of pyrotechnical splendor. As the sun imperceptibly slipped deeper into the junction of earth and sky behind the island the spectrum took on a subtle change, growing deeper, richer, less sparkling, and yet more intense in its color. It was as if the sky, suddenly realizing that the sun was actually leaving it, was changing from an ostentatious exhibition to a profound demonstration of emotion.

Susan turned to Michael, her heart full. "You couldn't have said good-bye in a more graphic way."

His arm tightened around her and she knew that the next moment he would be kissing her. But just at that moment Billy entered from the tiny cabin behind them with a service cart bearing a remarkable assortment of canapes and appetizers. There were tiny finger sandwiches, miniature crab quiches, and hot shrimp dip with crackers and celery sticks, stuffed cherry tomatoes, cheese wedges, cold meats, fresh fruits, a cheese and coconut dip for apple slices, and much, much more.

Susan laughed. "Now that's what you get for buying all the tickets. We'll each have to eat for six!"

And with the stiff sea air to boost their appetites, and recorded island music and the slowly fading sunset to provide atmosphere, they very nearly did just that.

At length Billy adjusted the sails and they skimmed the now dark waters toward shore. As they approached land the lights ringing the bay began to twinkle and dance on the water like diamonds on black velvet. A very different jewel display from the one they saw earlier, but stunning in its austerity.

The cruise was over but they were both reluctant for the evening to end. They walked for some time on the beach before slowly turning their steps toward the hotel. Outside her room they paused. "I'll be back in a few weeks, Susan. It isn't long until the convention, and I promised Kele I'd serve as groomsman for their wedding."

She nodded, afraid to speak.

He took her in his arms and his kiss was unspeakably gentle. Even as his arms tightened around her with fervor, his lips caressed her as if the moment were too significant for passion.

And then he was gone. He was gone and she was

alone. Destitute. For a long time she stood in her unlighted room: not thinking, not feeling, just being.

And then despondency broke through.

It wasn't fair. It was another of God's tricks—one of His little jokes to harass her. After her world fell apart she had decided there wasn't a God. Now she knew there was—one who delighted in tormenting her.

And yet even as she railed she knew that without his faith Michael would be less a person, less a man, less the one she loved.

She cried out to the emptiness of her room, "No! No, I don't! I can't! I won't!" not even sure what she meant by the denial.

She picked up a book lying on the table and threw it across the room. It didn't break anything, but it landed with a satisfying crash. She had a terrible urge to go on throwing things—to smash the room just as her world had been smashed.

CHAPTER 9

ROUTINE DESCENDED. THE HOURS SEEMED to drag and yet the days passed in an endless round of work. Michael did not call.

It was the little things she remembered. The crinkles at the corners of his gentle eyes when he smiled at her with—with adoration? It had seemed so at the time. His supreme kindness and patience— even when she was caustic, or angry, or even drunk; warmth flooded her face and she hung her head at the memory. The way he held her hand with such strength and assurance when she had been terrified for Kele and Lani. Laughing as they ran through the botanical gardens, kissing in the waterfall pool, sitting in quiet exultation under the majestic canopy of the sunset.

Oh, Michael.

"No, no Lani! I *told* you to put the Philadelphia bankers on the front page," Susan snapped, pointing at the *Aloha* lay-out in front of her.

Lani's large brown eyes looked at her with hurt and confusion.

"Oh, I'm sorry," Susan said with a sigh. "It just seems that everything is going wrong."

"That's all right, Miss Susan," Lani said softly. "I'll fix it awiwi."

"Yes, *very* fast, please. We should have had it at the printer's yesterday."

The phone rang and Lani picked it up for her, "Miss Jamison's office. . . . Yes. . . . One minute please." She put her hand over the mouthpiece and said to Susan, "It's a Mr. Joshua Nichols. . . ."

Susan stifled a small scream and buried her head in her hands. Then she took the receiver. "Oh, Josh, I'm so sorry! The time just got away from me. This is awful! I'll be right there." How could she possibly have forgotten to meet Josh at the airport?

"No, never mind, I'll rent a car. It'll be quicker. See ya in a few minutes, Susie."

When he hung up Susan leaned back in her chair and closed her eyes. She couldn't believe that had happened. Josh had been calling her almost every day for three weeks now. When she couldn't satisfy him with her vague replies to his demands that she come home, he announced that he was coming to her. There it was—arrival time and flight number neatly recorded on the desk calendar in front of her. Of course the morning had been hectic, and her mind was admittedly elsewhere, but this was really embarrassing. And disappointing—she had planned to meet him at the airport in traditional style with a lei and everything. Josh was her only hope for forgetting Michael, and she had to try to put her life back on an even footing. She couldn't go through the rest of her days not really caring whether or not she combed her hair in the morning.

She refreshed her lipstick, sprayed a breath of perfume on each side of her neck, and lightly brushed the shoulders of the little blue linen jacket that topped

136

her striped sun dress. She sat for a moment looking at the stripes in varying widths of color running across her lap. This was the same dress she had worn her first morning to work. The day she met Michael.

Well, that was over and the quicker forgotten the better. She rolled her memories of Michael in a tight little ball, stuffed it deep down inside her, stomped on it, and firmly padlocked it. There now! She rose with a determined gesture and walked to the lobby to await Josh's arrival.

"What kind of a place are you running here?" Josh fumed after giving her the briefest of kisses. "I asked the doorman if I should park the car myself. He said, 'You wanna park the car, you park it. You want me to park the car, I'll park it.' Then I said I wanted help with my bags, and he set them on the sidewalk! Don't you have any routine here?"

Susan laughed, "Easy, Josh. You're in the tropics now, you have to learn to hang loose." She held up her right hand, her three middle fingers curled under, thumb and pinkie extended, and waved it at him.

"And just what is that supposed to mean?"

"It's the local greeting, practically a symbol of the island. It means, 'Hang loose, brother.'"

Josh was obviously not in the mood for acquiring local customs. "I'm lucky I got here at all. I waited for my inter-island flight for over an hour. Then someone finally got around to telling me it had been cancelled. When I took my ticket to the airline desk, the attendant just wrote a new number on it. I asked if I was confirmed and she assured me, 'Oh, yes. You're confirmed.' She didn't check a computer or anything. For all she knew, that flight could have been oversold. I've never seen such inefficiency."

"*Was* it oversold?"

"I don't know. I made sure I was at the front of the line. I didn't have any intention of spending anymore time in that dumpy airport, I can tell you that."

"Go change into something cooler and we'll have a drink by the pool. Then you'll feel better," Susan urged, anxious to change the subject.

It took more than one drink, but Josh did seem to relax a bit as they sat behind the manmade waterfall by the pool. Their waiter had the black hair, olive skin, and laughing brown eyes so familiar on the island, but he was unusually tall and thin. His black hair was beginning to gray at the temples, making him appear much older than the other waiters.

"What nationality are you?" Josh asked, as the waiter brought his second cocktail.

A broad smile lighted the man's face, "American, sir," he said proudly, then departed.

Susan stifled her laugh just in time. But the humor was lost on Josh.

"I see you're still Miss PR—for Perfect Reputation," Josh said, eyeing her tall glass of lemoned iced tea.

Susan shrugged. "My reputation could very well become the hotel's reputation in the minds of guests. There are lots of jobs where one's private life isn't that private. You didn't mind in San Francisco."

"I wouldn't mind *now*, if you were in San Francisco—that's what I've come to talk about, you know."

When Susan didn't reply, Josh changed the subject.

"I was hoping we could go swimming this afternoon," he said leaning across the table toward Susan. "But this weather doesn't look too favorable. What would you like to do?"

"Several guests have asked me about the ancient Hawaiian Village, and I haven't seen it, so it's hard to answer their questions. We might go there. Or there's a new shopping arcade just up the street if you want to get some souvenirs for your nephews and that new niece."

Josh thought that was a good suggestion, as his

sister's three sons would expect something wonderful from Uncle Josh.

The shops were built in a U-shape in an attractive open air design with a covered boardwalk taking the shoppers from one store to the next. The center of the market area was filled with shady trees, tables for eating snacks, a dais for the daily hula show, and more small shops.

Susan and Josh went from shop to shop, looking at the display of native crafts in each one. Oriental imports were very popular and some of the stores offered lovely pieces of imported art work. It seemed that every third shop was a clothing store. And sea shell crafts abounded everywhere. Josh shook his head at Susan's suggestion of taking his nephews the brightly colored dragon kites she saw decorating the ceiling of one shop. "I know who'd get stuck assembling the things," Josh said.

He bought a lei of tiny pink silk flowers for his tiny pink niece and a doll in a grass skirt to give her later. "Don't let her have it until she's old enough not to eat the grass," advised Susan.

Then they spotted a tee shirt shop in the center of the market area. It offered hand painted, original design shirts and Josh decided that would be a safe choice for his nephews—no assembly required. They chose a different surfing pattern for each boy and were about to leave when Susan spotted a little pink shirt with a hand-painted orchid on it. "Oh, look at this, Josh, isn't it darling? You take it to Carol from me."

But then they realized they had three gifts for baby sister and only one for each boy. It took a while to locate swim goggles in junior sizes, but they finally concluded their shopping satisfactorily. They passed a small pastry shop emitting seductive scents and Josh bought a bag of almond cookies. They sat at one of the round tables next to a red-blossomed bush and nibbled the cookies. Fat little brown birds with blue beaks and legs and even blue eyelids hopped under the tables pecking at crumbs. Susan broke off bits of her cookie and tossed the crumbs to the birds. In spite of the overcast sky it was a pleasant afternoon. The splashing of water from the fountain near the dais, the chirping of birds in the trees, the muted sounds of the shoppers strolling along the boardwalk, made a pleasant backdrop for their conversation. But they didn't seem to have an awful lot to say.

Susan smiled at Josh. "It's great to see you, Susie," he said. "Are you glad I've come?"

"Of course," she replied. And she sturdily told herself that she meant it, too.

The afternoon hula show to attract camera-wielding tourists was beginning on the dais. With a flush of embarrassment, Susan recalled the hula show following the luau. "I really need to get back and finish up a few details at my desk, Josh. Was there anything else you wanted to shop for?"

"That looks like a nice jewelry store over there. Let's take a look on the way out."

Susan almost demurred, hoping he wasn't hinting about looking at diamond rings, but was quickly relieved to see his interest was in a shell necklace, which he thought would be a nice gift for his sister's birthday next month.

"These are Niihau shell leis from the Forbidden Island," the pareau-clad shop girl explained, bringing out a velvet tray of exquisite necklaces for his approval. "The shells are all gathered by Niihau islanders, graded according to color and size, and strung by hand, in a variety of patterns."

Susan was fascinated by the exquisite colors and patterns of the delicate shells. The clerk held out a multi-strand necklace with the shells strung end on end. "This is called a Sweetheart Lei. They are traditionally exchanged by the bride and groom at Niihua weddings. And these," she picked up a beautiful strand of red and hot pink shells, "are the rarest of all. Shells of these colors number only about one in five thousand, making them extremely valuable.

"Very nice," agreed Josh. "How much is that one?"

The girl turned over a small tag attached to the necklace. "This one is five thousand dollars," she said.

"Thank you," Josh replied. "We'll think about it." And taking Susan's arm, he ushered her out of the shop. "That's ridiculous! Seashells can't be worth that. Obviously a tourist trap. Catering to people who want to brag about how much they paid for things. And what is all this nonsense about a forbidden island, anyway?"

It had begun to rain while they were inside, but like all rains Susan had experienced since coming to Kauai, it was a bright rain. Even though the sky was cloudy, she still needed her sun glasses for comfort. "It's not far off the west coast of Kauai," she answered, putting on her dark glasses. "On a clear day you can see it from shore. Anyway, it's privately owned and is populated exclusively by native Hawaiians. Admittance is strictly forbidden to all but residents of Niihua. It's the last hold-out of the simple island life of long ago. There are about two-hundred-and-fifty residents, I think, and they mostly raise cattle and sheep."

"And make seashell necklaces," added Josh with a note of animosity in his voice. "And they really live there like that all the time?"

Susan nodded, "I guess so. That's what I've read."

Josh shook his head, "Drop-outs. Can't face civilization. What's the value of keeping ancient customs if no one can see them?"

"I assume the purpose is for the people who live there to be happy," she said, fighting to control her tone. She didn't want to fight with Josh. Certainly not over something so remote as this. But, how could *she* have said so many biting things to Michael? What was the matter with her? Suddenly she didn't like herself at all. But Josh was still haranguing.

"More likely to provide money for the owners of the island." He paused. "Hey, are there any good night clubs here? I want to take you out in style tonight."

The Beach Club and Boogie Palace was the most widely advertised night spot on the island, so Susan suggested it and dressed accordingly.

While getting ready she was mulling over the past hours with Josh. It had been so long since they'd been together, she almost felt as if they were strangers getting acquainted. He was even more handsome than she remembered, and yet, it had never occurred to her before that perhaps his jawline wasn't quite strong enough. She had never seen him so up-tight before, either. Or was it just that it didn't show in the sophisticated setting of San Francisco? Oh, well, maybe tonight would be different. But the truth of the matter was that Josh just didn't seem to be as much fun to be with as she remembered. Or was it the contrast? *In spite of being a Christian, Michael—or, was it because of being a Christian?—was so much fun, such an incomparable companion.* She refused to answer that and turned her full concentration on dressing for the evening.

She loved the feel of the lavender, satin-laced crepe tunic with butterfly sleeves that she slipped on over her head. Humming to herself, she pulled on matching straight legged pants and wrapped her slim waist in a

142

wide sash that was lavender on one side and ice blue on the other. She considered doing her hair up in a pile of curls, but was afraid a night in the Boogie Palace might be too much for that intricate hairstyle, so instead took a thick strand of hair from each side of her face and caught them with a wide pearl comb on the back of her head. Her eyes sparkled at the results.

At the tapping sound Susan smiled and flew to answer Michael's knock. Halfway across the room she froze in horror. *Michael's* knock? No wonder she was feeling so happy—her traitorous subconscious had tricked her into thinking she was dressing to go out with Michael.

She stood there while the knocking grew more insistent. She couldn't go through with it. She couldn't let another man touch her when her heart belonged to Michael. But Michael didn't want it; he was home with Heather. It was as if the package had been stamped, "refused, return to sender." But once bestowed it could never be returned, so her heart had wound up in the dead letter office. Forcing her feet to move and her lips to smile she opened the door.

"Wow! What a knock-out!" Josh leered at her, and she was relieved to know that at least her pretense didn't show.

Josh ordered champagne to open the evening. The music was loud and the tables were set too close together for intimate dining, but the food was delicious. At least it would have been delicious if Susan's battered emotions hadn't turned it to cotton in her mouth.

Josh kept the champagne glasses full and since it was too noisy in the room for conversation, Susan concentrated on trying to eat and drink. She had learned her lesson on the Mai Tais, however, so she took only tiny sips of the champagne. She noted, though, that Josh was not being so restrained.

For dessert Josh ordered Naughty Hula Pie—a sinful concoction of chocolate crumb crust, macadamia nut ice cream, chopped macadamia nuts, and hot fudge sauce. He pressed Susan to order a piece too, but she chose passion fruit chiffon pie instead. Maybe a little of it could slide past the lump in her throat.

The chiffon filling was a safe choice but a bite of the pie crust was her undoing. A crumb of it refused to slide. She coughed, choked, and her eyes blurred with tears. The crumb went down leaving her with a sore throat, watery eyes, and a distaste for flaky pie crusts. The hovering waiter refilled her water glass and she sipped slowly, giving herself time to regain her composure.

This was ridiculous! Missing Michael so much she couldn't even eat was more than she intended to put up with. Michael was gone and apparently had lost his appetite for her. Josh was here, wanting to show her a good time. And she would have a good time—even if she had to be miserable doing it!

The boogie room was in a separate building across the grounds. The loud music in the dining room was only there to whet their appetites for what was to come. It had rained during dinner and the walkway was deeply puddled. They were just about to walk around a golf cart, inexplicably parked right in front of the door, when the driver helped an elderly couple aboard and called to Susan and Josh to jump on too. "Going to boogie?" he asked.

They nodded, not sure they wanted to get on the vehicle.

"That's where we're headed," said the grey-haired gentleman passenger. "Come on!"

It would have been rude to refuse, so they perched on the back and held on. Susan looked up at the pink and white striped canvas top, thinking it was too picturesque to be real. Then the whole thing roared into life and took off with a jerk. Unfortunately, rainwater had pooled on the canvas awning, and the rapid start dislodged it, sending it sloshing all over Josh's pantlegs. Susan heard him swearing under his breath, but she was biting her lips so hard to keep from laughing that she could offer no comfort to calm him down.

When they alighted from the cart, after having hung on for dear life around several harrowing curves, Susan could no longer contain herself. Her over-wrought emotions broke and she laughed until tears streamed from her eyes, streaking the mascara she'd put on for the evening.

"I fail to see the humor in the situation!" Josh snarled, surveying the damp cuffs hanging around his ankles. "This whole island is unforgivably disorganized. Like when we first got here," he recounted. "You saw what happened—I parked in a nice open spot with no 'no parking' signs to be seen, and that policeman came up and told me I couldn't park there! Then I was driving around looking for another place—with no 'one way' signs anywhere and the same policeman tells me I'm going the wrong way! Now this!"

Josh's anger helped Susan get her hysteria under control as she realized she was just antagonizing him. She was trembling and felt light headed. Her voice was thin and forced. "Well, they may be disorganized, but they're sure friendly. Now come on, let's boogie."

If the music in the restaurant had been loud, this was deafening. The room was bathed in a hot pink light and the floor was crowded with couples gyrating uninhibitedly to the clamorous strains. Josh took Susan's hand and led her onto the floor. The fleeting thought crossed Susan's mind that this wouldn't be Michael's kind of place. The thought stiffened her resolution to have a good time. Picking up the beat of the music—which was no problem since the room was vibrating with it—Susan determinedly began dancing with Josh.

They had barely started when the musicians began a new number, faster in tempo than the first, and the lights began flashing red, green, gold, and blue.

The next number was less cacophonous, and the lights were dimmed to a pale blue candlelight glow. Josh clasped Susan to him and whirled her around the room, her feet barely touching the floor. He was holding her much too close for decorum or comfort, but she didn't protest.

Later she could not sort out the dances in her mind. The whole evening seemed a whirling melange of noise and lights and writhing bodies. She could hardly even remember Josh, although she could picture his curly brown hair tossing above her when she looked up at him. She could remember his hot, insistent kiss later when they were in the car. He had even been pressing about his desire to come up to her room with her—something he had never done in San Francisco after she once made her refusal absolutely clear.

She put him off with the most tactful excuses she could manufacture and when she was finally alone in her room the silence was stunning. She walked out onto her lanai and took deep breaths of the fresh sea air, allowing her inner turbulence to be calmed by the rhythm of the ocean on the shore.

And then, as always, when she was quite relaxed, Michael came to her in her thoughts. The only compensation for her pain was the thought that at least he didn't know how much she cared. But if he didn't care, how did she explain all those times . . .

He was probably interested in her soul, she thought bitterly. What a laugh she would have had about that before she met Michael. But now it ceased to be a laughing matter.

But Michael couldn't be interested in the real her. There was all that stuff in the Bible about not being unequally yolked together, and Michael would certainly want a good little pious wife. Someone like Heather undoubtedly was. He would never become unequally yolked with someone who had chosen skepticism over hypocrisy.

And then her carefully held emotions engulfed her, flooding over her like the traumatic crashing of a breaking wave. She loved him so much. In spite of everything he stood for—everything she said she would never have anything to do with, everything she despised as sham, fanatacism, narrowness . . .

She loved him. She was horrified by how just the thought of him could make her ache. But at the same time an even greater horror engulfed her. He didn't love her. He was attracted to her, he enjoyed her company, she had enlivened his vacation and would be there for his convention but . . .

That was it! She must *not* be here when he came back. She would tell Josh he had won. She'd resign.

It had been a terrible night after her emotional storm, but the next morning Susan was determined to face the day—and life—like the realist she prided herself on being. Since the sun was shining, Josh suggested it would be a good chance for her visit to Kamokila, the reconstructed ancient village she mentioned the day before.

Susan relaxed in the car next to Josh, returning his smiles and making no objection to his putting an arm around her. It was just like old times. Almost. The road down into the village which had been built a few years before on the tree-lined banks of the wide blue Wailua River was steep, bumpy, and curving. Susan clung to the edge of her seat as the little car bounced its way down. But once they were there the village spread out in repose on its wide green carpet—a peaceful, level valley nestled at the foot of a forested mountain.

The village consisted of nineteen huts built of materials from the valley—red guava wood, rocks, and river pebbles. The roofs were thatched with cane leaves. The warm sun shone on the little clearing and Susan, who always liked to give play to her active imagination, went from hut to hut picturing the village alive with happy, smiling, brown-skinned children, the sun shining on their fat little tummies as they romped through the village, disturbing their elders who were busy cooking fish over open fires, pounding taro root into poi, weaving lauhala leaves into mats, and making ti-leaf skirts. She even imagined a shy young couple emerging from the honeymoon hut after spending the night on the flat slabs of rock placed there for their wedding night. And then she saw the men returning from a successful fish spearing party and retiring to their separate eating lodge, to be served by the women.

Susan started to comment on the romance of it all, which seemed heightened to her by the fact that the reconstruction was on the site of an actual Hawaiian village, but her thoughts were cut short when Josh commented, "You don't plan to recommend this to your guests, do you? I don't suppose they need to endure that road down here just to see that the early islanders were primitive and uncivilized."

"I think it's very interesting," Susan returned quietly. "I'm glad we came."

"Well, that's good, anyway. I'm glad *you* enjoyed it. Now for tonight, since the weather is cooperating, how would you like to go on a sunset cocktail cruise on a catamaran?"

Susan gasped. She couldn't possibly relive those moments alone with Michael in that incredible world of color that still burned in her memory. "Thank you,

Josh. But I'd prefer something on dry land if you don't mind."

"Really? That's the first time I ever knew you suffered from seasickness. But that's fine, whatever you want."

In the end they ate at the Langford and then walked on the beach until Susan could truthfully claim fatigue when Josh started dropping hints about going to her room with her. In all, it had been a rather pleasant day, Susan mused as she treated herself to a long bubble bath before retiring.

The next day was Sunday and she blissfully slept late. Even later than she really meant to, since Josh was taking her to a champagne brunch at a rival hotel. She had been hearing about this brunch, which was becoming famous on the island, and she was anxious to experience it.

And indeed, it was an experience. Susan had been to many elegant brunches and buffets in San Francisco, but never anything like this. An overwhelming number of tables were banked with orchids and other tropical flowers as a background for the gourmet delights they offered. After being shown to their tables by a hostess in a long flowered dress, Susan and Josh chose to tackle first the table of hot dishes: Clam pasta, sweet and sour spare ribs, Portuguese sausage, Eggs Benedict. . . .

Even taking only a sampling of each offering, Susan could see she would never make it through the course. Josh went next to the made-to-order omelets, but Susan chose to sit that one out.

By the time they went together to the third table they were laughing helplessly.

They had been eating for more than an hour and had sampled less than half of the delicacies.

Susan sat with just a cup of tea while Josh made his way around the tables of salads. With Michael firmly out of Susan's mind, they had a marvelous time. The more they ate the worse their jokes got, but the funnier they seemed. The tensions Susan had felt with Josh ever since his arrival seemed completely dissolved, and since there was nothing here for Josh to complain about in the way of service or civilization, he was a charming companion.

At last they made their way slowly to the gardens bordering the beach, determined to walk the breakfast off. "At least we laughed a lot," said Susan. "That's supposed to be great for digestion."

They took off their shoes and walked on the sand away from the hotel until they found a secluded spot. Josh turned to her, serious now. "Susan, I have to go back in a few hours. I wish you could come with me. I can't go on without you much longer. Surely you know that."

She took a deep breath. Now was the time. She had to do it. She had steeled herself for it, practically rehearsed it. "Yes, Josh, I know. I've decided to resign my job like you want."

"Susan, that's wonderful!" He grabbed her and kissed her. There was nothing unpleasant about Josh's kisses, but Susan knew they could never do to her what Michael's did.

"When? How soon can you do it?"

"There's really nothing to wait for. I'll type out my resignation as soon as I get back to the office. But, Josh, I won't leave until I've found a replacement." She was firm about that.

"I understand. That's fine, Susie. Just so it's definite. And now, just one more little detail." He reached in his pocket and pulled out a small jeweler's box.

Susan gasped when she saw the size of the diamond he held out to her—a pear-shaped solitaire set in a slim band of white gold. It was almost blinding when the sun caught it. Susan held out her left hand, trembling, and Josh slipped the ring on. It was stunning; it was fabulously valuable; it was cold-looking.

When they arrived back at the hotel there was little time left. Josh went up to his room to close his bags while Susan, true to her decision, went to her office and typed out her resignation, effective as soon as a replacement could be found, signed it, sealed it in an envelope, and put it on Ted's desk.

There was just time for a brief farewell in the lobby before Josh hurried off to catch his plane. Susan refused to admit she was relieved not to have to go through a long passionate leave-taking. She turned and walked quickly down the marble hallway, not noticing the "caution wet floor" signs left there by the cleaning crew. Her foot caught a wet puddle and she fell down hard and painfully on the stone surface with a sharp cry.

"Oh, Miss Jamison, we are so sorry." Two white-jacketed boys from housekeeping flew to her side still carrying their mops.

She wasn't seriously hurt, but she was furious. Here was her chance to vent her anger at the whole world. "Why can't you be more careful!" she cried, pointing to small pools of water down the hall. "It looks like you stumbled when you carried the bucket!" And with that she stormed off, leaving the cleaning crew truly stuttering their apologies.

She marched unseeing to her room and slammed the door behind her. It was several moments before her mind registered the fact that room service had made a delivery while she was out. A large white florist box lay on her table. She tore the lid off, amazed that Josh could have had flowers delivered in such a short time.

She was stunned by the sight that greeted her from the box—a spray of the deep red/black velvet orchids that so far as she knew grew only by the waterfall pool. The simple white card had only one mark on it—"M."

She dropped into a chair, her head in her hands. She had tried to do the right thing. She had tried to escape Michael's haunting memory. But now she knew she couldn't kill her love with denial. She couldn't even muzzle it. She would seal it up one place and it would spring out another like a leaky dam.

She stared for a long time at the ring on her finger, then raised her head and looked at herself in the mirror across the room. What had she done?

CHAPTER 10

"AND WHAT IS YOUR PREVIOUS experience?" Susan asked the nervous blond girl sitting in front of her desk.

"I worked as a waitress at the Marine Cafe while I was in high school. And since graduation I've been a secretary for an insurance company. And of course, I've done a lot of babysitting," she added hopefully.

Susan suppressed twin impulses to laugh and cry when the girl left. The situation was hopeless. That earnest child was the best applicant she'd had in almost two weeks of interviewing. Ted had been understandably upset when he found Susan's resignation on his desk, but accepted it as inevitable when she showed him her ring. "Just remember I'm relying on you to find a qualified replacement," he said. "Of course, I'll be responsible for the final hiring, but I want you to handle the interviewing and training."

Lani's reaction to Susan's announcement had been one of bewilderment. Susan knew how much Lani and Kele thought of Michael and was sure they had expected Susan to be wearing his ring soon. But Lani was so caught up in the bliss of planning her own wedding—just three days away now—that nothing really penetrated her bubble of euphoria.

". . . And the dresses are all finished. I saw them last night. They are so beautiful." She gave a dreamlike sigh. "I can't wait to wear my gown for Kele. And you and Alika will be lovely in yours." She hugged Susan impulsively. "Only three more days!" And then she became very serious. "I am so grateful . . . if you and Mr. Travis hadn't helped us . . ."

Susan smiled and returned the hug, "I know, Lani. Now don't even think about it. Seeing your happiness at the wedding will be our joy too." Susan could always smile and say the right thing—it was part of her professional training. But she knew the wedding would be an agony for her. Lani's sister, Alika, was to be Maid of Honor, and Susan, bridesmaid. She remembered Michael telling her just before he left that Kele had asked him to be groomsman. That would put them side-by-side for the ceremony. Well, she would just have to get through it somehow.

"Mr. Rawlings said I could have the afternoon off. I have to check with the florist and the boat people and so many details . . . if there's nothing more you need?"

Susan realized Lani was waiting for an answer. "Oh, no, that'll be fine. Have a nice afternoon, Lani. I'm sure everything will be perfect."

When Lani left, Susan found her mind as full of the wedding as the bride's. She tried to picture herself standing beside Michael in the Fern Grotto, which was often called the most romantic spot on earth. Standing beside the man she loved while wearing another man's ring. How could she possibly go through with it? She tried to force her thoughts back to the details of a large banquet the Langford was catering next week. She heard her door open but didn't look up, supposing Lani had come back for something she had forgotten.

"Miss Jamison?"

A small, nondescript young woman in a pale blue dress brought Susan's attention back to the present. "Yes, may I help you?"

"I'm Heather Daniels, with CLA."

Heather? *This* was Heather? The woman she had envisioned stealing Michael's affections with her captivating beauty and charm? "Oh, yes, *Heather!*" In a flood of relief, Susan couldn't resist jumping to her feet and hugging the startled girl. "I'm so glad you've come!"

Heather blinked in surprise, but replied with poise. "I'm delighted to be here. There aren't any problems about the convention are there?"

"Oh, no, none at all—yet. But my experience has taught me that five days before the convention is too soon to count your chickens. Anyway, with my secretary lost in wedding plans, your assistance will be invaluable in double checking details. I believe Mi . . . er, Mr. Travis said you'd be handling the registration and arrangements for CLA?"

Susan felt she was babbling, but fortunately Heather had taken her warm greeting as simply relief over having help with the convention work. "There is a small desk right through here where you can work." Susan led the way. "This afternoon we can go over the arrangements for speakers' rooms together."

Heather's desk was in a room next to Susan's where she covertly watched the girl going about settling in. Although Susan had covered her emotions she was still fluttering inside—this couldn't possibly be her rival. Heather was obviously a person to be described as "sweet", but except for the bounce and shine to her plain brown hair and a warm glow of

155

tranquility in her pale blue eyes—Susan felt catty thinking it—she could be described as decidedly mousy.

After working with Heather for less than twenty-four hours, however, Susan was forced to revise her opinion. The inkling of jealousy Susan was beginning to feel for Heather was based on far more than the way the girl always referred to Michael on a first name basis in her lovely soft voice. Susan sat on her lanai the next evening after work, trying to analyze her reaction to Heather. Being around Heather was like being in the soft glow of a candle—warm, gentle, gracious.

Susan thought how Heather related to everyone on the staff with thoughtful courtesy—it was as if she possessed a special brand of love. With a pang, Susan realized she had met that quality before: her mother, her pastor's wife when Susan was a child, a few long-lost friends at church—people far gone from her life since reality and cynicism intervened. Susan sat for a long time, watching the sea roll on the sands beyond the hotel lawn, almost lapping the feet of the swaying palms growing along the edge of the beach. Finally she sighed and let in the thought that had been hammering for admittance: Her list wasn't complete—Michael, too, possessed that special quality of love.

And with that acknowledgment came also the realization of its lack in her own life. Susan understood that the feeling she had been interpreting as jealousy of Heather was really a feeling of inadequacy of this special quality in herself. She had once known it—a love she had received and then been able to give to others—long ago before she turned her back on it. Was she happier then? She wondered. But before she could answer that she was engulfed with the awful knowledge that Heather could give this love to

156

Michael. It was what he deserved, but Susan wanted to be the one to give it to him.

The next morning, Susan and Heather were seated on opposite sides of Susan's desk going over the interminable details to be arranged for the convention. Susan knew that in San Francisco much of this could have been left to the staff in the various departments, but this was the first large convention for the Langford Kauai and her staff was yet to be tested by the fire of experience.

"You'd better double check with catering to be sure they have twenty-nine VIP baskets made up, then be sure housekeeping has the right number of rooms for all those who are to receive turn-down service with candy on their pillows at night. Be sure they have the name right, too, because the letters of welcome from the manager are personalized—it would rather spoil the effect if they were delivered to the wrong rooms. . . ." Susan dictated and Heather checked the items off her list. "And of course, check the arrangements for Governor Bradshaw's arrival and housing with his security staff—we don't want any hitches there."

"I'll also want to be sure the staff is prepared for mass arrivals of guests," Susan continued. "Do your registration forms indicate time of arrival?"

Heather nodded and efficiently pulled a file from her brief case. "It looks like one hundred and thirty will arrive the night before, mostly on the six o'clock flight, some on the eight-thirty; two hundred will be in after breakfast the next morning, and the other one hundred twenty-five before the keynote luncheon."

Susan sat in stunned silence, hoping she'd misunderstood. "Wait a minute, that adds up to over four hundred and fifty registrants! We had been told you expected three hundred."

157

Heather smiled. "Yes, we were rather overwhelmed at the response ourselves. It must have been your color brochures of the hotel."

"But we're an out-island—all our supplies have to come from the big island or from the mainland!" With a sinking feeling, Susan reached for the phone and pushed the button for catering; but before they could answer, the door flung open, and a very large, dark man strode across the room and slammed his heavy fist on Susan's desk.

"There's been a security leak! This could put the governor's life in jeopardy—what are you going to do about it?"

"But that's impossible," Susan protested. "Only Ted Rawlings and I know which room Governor Bradshaw is to occupy. It couldn't have leaked."

"Nevertheless, I caught a newsman sneaking around his suite," the governor's security chief growled at her. "It got out somehow, and it's your job to correct it."

Susan nodded in agreement; the Governor of Washington who was noted for his stand on keeping his state's school rooms available for such groups as Youth for Christ and Young Life to have after-school meetings, was to deliver the keynote address to the convention—and security was her responsibility.

The guard impatiently drummed his fingers on her desk as Susan's brain sought for a method to handle this delicate problem; but before she could even discard her first unworkable idea, Heather, who had been on the phone to the front desk said, "Susan, Cranston Adams, the big trial lawyer from Boston just arrived. The suite we reserved for him is totally inadequate—I knew he was bringing his family, but I had no idea he had *seven* children!"

"I'm so sorry to bother you," Lani entered in her quiet, graceful way, "but the committee from the

American Medical Association is here to make plans for next year's convention. They are demanding to see you now because they only allotted one day to stay on Kauai."

It flashed through Susan's mind that she must be going crazy—she had seen plays with scenes like this where everything hit the fan, but she'd never imagined it could happen in real life. Suppressing a terrible urge to dissolve in laughter, she gripped the edge of her desk and managed to say, "Take them to lunch on the house, Lani, then have them talk to catering about meals. I'll try to join them after that."

"Yes, Miss Susan, and . . ." She hesitated.

"Is there something else, Lani?"

"Well, just that the videotape you requested for showing at your speech to the Rotary Club this evening hasn't arrived."

"Thank you, Lani," she replied weakly as Lani departed, and she mechanically reached for the call coming in on her direct line from Ted's office.

"About the governor's security . . ." The guard was growing impatient.

"They put champagne in the VIP baskets," Heather announced, turning again from her phone.

"We've got a problem here, Susan," Ted's voice came down the wire sounding tight with nerves.

"Welcome to the club," Susan quipped.

"This is no joking matter! Are you alone, Susan?"

"No, just a minute." She put Ted on hold and turned to the harried faces in her office. "Heather, tell them to take out the champagne and put in Perrier. If you'll have a seat in the reception room, Mr. Norris, I'll be with you in a minute," she told the security officer in a voice that brooked no arguing.

"Okay, Ted. I'm alone."

"You sitting down, Susan? Sergeant Johnson just called from the big island—he has reason to believe that group we have registered as the Pacific Orchid Growers Association is actually the Polynesian Liberation Corps and may be planning a public demonstration.''

Susan closed her eyes and took three deep breaths. This must be the moment all her training and experience had prepared her for—or at least she'd soon know if she was prepared. A tiny voice in the back of her head whispered that it would help if she could call on wiser and stronger help than her own resources, but she quickly stifled that idea.

''Okay, Ted,'' she replied in a voice that sounded a calm she was far from feeling, ''you'll have to call the attorney general in Honolulu to get permission to refuse them service on the grounds that they are known to carry guns and could endanger our guests and staff—we don't want a stink in the press for interfering with someone's constitutional right to peaceful assembly. Then you can have Sergeant Johnson's men and hotel security remove them, but see that they do it *quietly*. The safety of our guests and the reputation of the hotel depend on it.''

In a voice less fraught with tension than it was earlier, Ted thanked her and hung up. Staring blankly at her desk, Susan wished she could feel relieved of tension. She had to come up with a plan for protecting the life of the Governor of the State of Washington, and she had to do it fast. She didn't like the responsibility. Security of hotel guests was her job, but the security breach hadn't come from her. If something happened to the Governor, how much of it would really be her fault?

She sat for several long moments with her head in her hands, elbows on her desk, concentrating on the problem. Her office door opened and heavy male footsteps crossed the room to her desk. She dropped her hands and looked up; her heart stopped; it wasn't the security officer. Just as on that first day so many weeks ago, she raised her eyes slowly up the well-tailored sports slacks and shirt to the gray eyes. But this time the eyes were not smiling. They were riveted on her left hand, which was resting on the desk in front of her. The cold eyes pierced her. She felt it with a stab of pain that drove all thoughts of convention confusions from her consciousness.

"What is the meaning of *that?"* His eyes were frigid as ice, hard as granite; his jaw was set and the bones of his face prominent with rigidly controlled anger.

There was no way she could answer his question, so she ignored it. "What are you doing here?" Susan asked in a weak voice.

"I came early so we could have some time together." Each word came separately as if it had been bitten off. "My mistake." He turned on his heel and left the room, but not before his mask slipped and Susan saw the pain under the anger. The cramp at her heart was so severe she doubled over.

The next invasion of her office brought Stan Norris and Heather, whose troubled eyes told Susan she had witnessed Michael's wrathful exit. "Please, have a seat," Susan said, clasping her hands tightly under her desk. "I think I can solve both your problems: We will put Mr. Adams and his brood in the suite reserved for the Governor—it's the largest in the hotel. If all the sofas are made up it will sleep ten. That should be adequate. Heather, will you please escort him there personally, but don't tell the front desk of the change."

Officer Norris gave Heather the keys to the room and Heather departed. "Now, Mr. Norris . . ." Susan studied the floor plan of the hotel. "Suite 907 is in a secure location away from elevators and stairways with no other rooms overlooking its balcony; we will put Governor Bradshaw there. We will also set up rooms 912 and 723 as decoys. The hotel will provide mock security, but the Governor will be expected to pay for the rooms. All room service orders should come from room 912 and then be carried to the Governor when there is no staff around. You and I, Mr. Norris are the only two people to know these room numbers. Is that satisfactory?"

The burly officer nodded curtly, "Most satisfactory, Miss Jamison."

Susan fought the desire to relax as soon as she was alone; she had to keep the adrenaline flowing until all problems were under control. She called the front desk to advise them of the swollen registration numbers—the rooms to be vacated by the "Pacific Orchid Growers" would come in handy, and if they weren't enough some guests would have to be accommodated at the neighboring hotels. That done, Lani returned in time to receive Susan's orders to prepare fifty publicity packets for her to hand out to the Rotarians in lieu of the absent audio visual materials, and, clipboard in hand, Susan went out to meet the American Medical Association contingent.

Only when the emergency was over could she allow herself to think of Michael. The following hours Susan lived in dread and in hope of seeing him again. She worried over what she would say, how she would look, how she would act. But it was all in vain. She didn't see him. . . .

Until that night when she tossed on her bed; and he stood before her again in her office. If all she had seen was his anger she could dismiss it as wounded ego and come to terms with it. But his pain she had felt as her own—because it was her own—and she couldn't handle that. The weight in her chest bore down until she thought she would suffocate but no amount of position changing or deep breathing could remedy it.

The fear was growing in her that she would have to live with this for the rest of her life. At first she was so sure she could will herself to be happy—to forget. But the weight was so much heavier than it had been just two weeks ago. What would two months do to her? Or two *years*? And the fact that the situation was of her own making made it all just that much worse.

In desperation she did something she hadn't done for years and years. Without conscious decision, almost as reflex left over from earlier days, she slipped to her knees beside her bed. "I've made such a mess of things. Just help me. Please help me."

Then she slept.

Lani's wedding day dawned bright and clear, as beautiful as Lani's smile and shining eyes. The temperamental spring weather of a few weeks ago was now behind them and they could enjoy the glories of early summer sunshine.

Susan and Alika helped Lani into her wedding gown of white organdy with a wide lace panel up the front, a Victorian-style ruffle over the shoulders, and a deep, lace-trimmed ruffle at the bottom of the skirt.

"Oh, Lani, you're the most beautiful bride I've ever seen!" exclaimed Susan. "That dress is perfect on you, especially the sleeves." The sleeves, which fit tight from shoulder to elbow, then fell to the wrist in deeply pointed triangles of lace, gave the dress a storybook quality.

Alika adjusted Lani's headpiece. She had chosen to wear a wreath of white roses around her head rather than a traditional veil. It was perfect on her sleek black hair. She carried no flowers, but in Hawaiian tradition she and Kele would exchange leis before the ceremony began.

Susan and Alika were wearing wreaths of pale pink roses in their hair. Their dresses were sleeveless versions of the bridal gown, Alika's in blue and Susan's in lilac. Susan was thankful for her short white gloves, which hid the diamond ring weighing on her hand and her heart.

They had dressed in Susan's room because the wedding party was to assemble at the hotel, then go by limousine to the boat that would take them up the river to the Fern Grotto. With pounding heart, Susan went down to meet the others.

She thought she had prepared herself. But nothing could have prepared her for her first sight of Michael in formal attire. The perfect fit of the black tuxedo emphasized his well-built height even more than swimming trunks had, and the gleaming white ruffled shirt accentuated his ruggedly handsome features and thick dark-gold hair. She grasped the edge of a planter until she could regain her composure.

He walked toward her, his face expressionless. "We don't want to spoil the day for the bridal couple, so we'll act as if nothing's happened. Right?" His words were as expressionless as his face, but nothing could blot out the grim lines around his mouth.

"Right," Susan agreed, and forced a small, stiff smile. He held out his arm, and she took it with her left hand, more thankful than ever for the glove covering it.

Kele introduced his cousin George who was to serve as his best man. Kele's father and Lani's mother, who were their only other relatives, would meet them at the dock.

The dock at the mouth of the wide, smooth Wiaulua river was buzzing with wedding guests and well-wishers. Now that all convention plans were running smoothly, many of the hotel staff had been given time off for the occasion, and Susan saw Ted Rawlings, a broad smile beaming below his bald head, among the familiar faces. The wedding party took seats in a special white boat decorated with ferns hanging all around the outside, and the guests followed in a sightseeing launch.

The bridal boat sailed up the busy river and Susan gave her attention to the activity outside, rather than to the man sitting so disturbingly close beside her in the cabin. There were jet boats with waterskiers, wind-surfers with colorful red and orange sails, mullet fishers working their nets, local children swimming—the sun shining on their little bronze bodies as they jumped off the river banks with shrieks of delight.

A breeze from the ocean ruffled the trees along the banks, making them sway like the motion of the water. The banks of the river were as heavily jungled as Susan would have imagined the Amazon to be, and even on this sunny day the water was shady from the verdant growth along the banks. Susan noted especially the tall bushes that grew in an almost solid wall with heart-shaped leaves and large, bright, red and orange flowers. She mentioned them to Michael, as much for something to say as anything.

"Yes," he agreed, "they are interesting. Each blossom has a one-day life span. It is red in the morning, orange in the afternoon, and yellow in the evening. That night they are found floating on the river. Since it's about noon now, some are red and some are orange."

He was being the perfect escort, making the trip more interesting by responding expansively to her comments. He couldn't have punished her as much by railing at her spitefully. All the times of enchantment they had shared exploring the island, all the little-known facts he'd taught her, all the intriguing wildlife he'd introduced her to . . . it was all there to haunt her with unfulfilled longings.

The boat wound its way upstream, past palm trees growing right out of the water, morning glory plants hanging in long vines from the trees, and egrets making their nests in high branches along the water's edge. At last they came to the dock and the boatman cut the engine. They were rocked gently by the waves as the little skiff was made secure.

The party was greeted at the dock by a flock of brightly feathered Bantam chickens, which George shooed out of the bride's way, and the merry party progressed up the path, which was like a tunnel beneath the spreading branches of banyan trees and other jungle growth, with bright torch ginger making flames of color in the intense greenery.

The procession paused when they rounded the steep path and came in view of the fairy-tale grotto. The sight was pure enchantment. A thin, feathery waterfall fell a hundred feet over the wide mouth of the opening. Single-frond ferns, some of them ten feet long, hung from the lava walls and ceiling of the cave like tinsel from a Christmas tree. And the jungle around the grotto caressed the scene in a green softness.

The guests arrived behind them, and as the musicians began soft strains of island music, Lani and Kele walked up the curved stone stairway into the natural cathedral under the ferns. Their attendants followed them, and a few of the guests chose to stand in the grotto with the bride and groom's parents while others stayed below the stairs on the terraced landing.

The bride and groom placed long rope leis of the traditional mailka leaves from Kauai's mountains around each other's necks. And then the musicians began the familiar strains of "The Hawaiian Wedding Song." Susan had heard it sung many times but never like this. The clarity of the girls' high tones, the mellow male voices, the gentle guitar strums, all blended in purity and perfection of harmony in this acoustically unsurpassed setting.

"I do love you with all my heart," the singers repeated back and forth to each other, and Susan's aching heart was crying the words to Michael. If only she hadn't made such a hopeless mess of things, maybe something could have worked out. Maybe . . . maybe. . . . But she shut her mind to what was impossible. Everything was impossible. With burning eyes and throat she forced her attention back to the familiar words spoken by the black-robed minister. "Dearly beloved, we are gathered here today in the sight of God and these witnesses to join together in holy matrimony. . . ."

Susan couldn't resist the impulse to look at Michael. She turned her head slowly, almost imperceptibly, then with a sharp intake of breath discovered why the impulse to look at him had been so strong—his gray eyes were focused on her. At first she couldn't understand the look in them. And then she knew. Michael's eyes were glistening with tears.

The realization was such a jolt that she blinked. When she looked back he was gazing straight forward, head up, dry-eyed. She must have imagined it. He couldn't possibly care that much, not after being gone all that time without writing or calling.

". . . You may kiss the bride." The ceremony was over. Susan was still holding tight to Michael's arm, much tighter than she realized, as they followed George and Alika out of the grotto, over a little stone bridge spanning a running stream, and through an area that was more parklike than the intense jungle the ascending trail had taken them through.

All the way back in the boat and all through the wedding dinner at the Langford, which was Ted's present to the newlyweds, Susan smiled and chatted and hoped desperately that she looked normal. But her mind was whirling with the searing questions going round and round. Could she ever go through that ceremony with Josh? Could she promise to love, honor, and cherish Josh until death did them part? The thought was ludicrous.

At last Kele and Lani led out in a bridal waltz and then, amid showers of rice and good wishes, slipped off to the honeymoon suite. Now Susan was free to escape to her room. Michael was on the other side of the room talking to Heather. Without a backward glance, Susan fled.

As soon as the door was shut behind her she ripped off her glove and pulled the ring viciously from her finger, scraping her knuckle mercilessly with her fingernails. In a frenzy she searched through her top drawer for the jeweler's box. In her agitation she must have passed it several times, for she finally had to yank the drawer out and dump the contents on the bed before she found the small blue and gold box.

She picked up the ring gingerly, as if it would burn her, and placed it in the satin-lined case. Still holding it, she sat down.

She fully realized that by this act she was condemning herself to a solitary life. She looked at the diamond winking at her from its satin bed. Being engaged to Josh hadn't accomplished the purpose for which she had embarked on it. Nothing would accomplish that purpose. She knew now that Michael Travis was as much a part of her as the air she breathed, and she'd never be free of his spell. But since nothing could ever come from those feelings—and she knew now she could never settle for a lesser man—she'd simply have to do without. With a defiant lift of her chin she snapped the lid shut. Tomorrow she would mail it.

CHAPTER 11

JUST BEFORE DARK THE DEPRESSION that had been growing on her all afternoon became overwhelming. She hadn't wanted to leave her room. She told herself it was because she wanted to be alone, although she knew it was because she didn't want to be out in case Michael should call. But he didn't call.

At last she decided to go for a walk on the beach before she started banging her head against the walls of her room. She slipped into white slacks and a pink tee shirt and made her way out a little-used door at the side of the hotel. A walk there led through landscaped grounds and down to the beach.

Lost in her thoughts, she didn't notice that some repair work was being done on the walk just ahead of her.

"I don't recommend walking in the wet cement." Michael's voice, coming out of nowhere, jolted her to a stop.

She looked at the patch of newly poured cement in front of her. "I wasn't planning on it," she said with a smile. Then she looked up. Her heart leaped at the sight of him. "But then, you never know, do you?"

"I was concerned," he grinned at her.

"I know. The lawyer's mind. 'There's precedent for it.'"

For the first time since his return, their smiles met and the wall between them shattered. In that moment his eye fell on her ringless hand. His hands clasped hers with joyful warm pressure that sent blood thrilling through her and filling her with an ecstasy that almost frightened her. *I mustn't, oh, I mustn't feel this way about him*, she cried silently. *What will I do when he's gone again?*

"Just one more day until the troops descend," he said. "How about a beach picnic tomorrow?"

There was no conflict, no weighing the consequences. She simply nodded. Forgetting all about her planned walk on the beach, she floated back to her room.

And the next morning she was still floating when she hurried down to the lobby to meet Michael. But the bubble burst with a resounding bang when Susan stepped around the fern-filled planter just in time to see Michael kissing Heather.

Even when they saw her they didn't pull apart, but walked toward her, their arms still around each other, wreathed in smiles.

"Congratulate me!" Heather cried, holding out her left hand with a gleaming ring as she beamed at Michael.

Susan opened her mouth obediently, but no words would come out. She told her feet to get out of there, but they wouldn't move. She just stood there frozen.

"Congratulate *her*?" Michael teased. "Better to congratulate *me*—she finally agreed to take the pest off my hands."

"How could I refuse after that wedding yesterday?'' Heather twinkled and Susan wondered how she could ever have thought the girl was mousy.

"Hey, what do you think you're doing, making time with my fiancée?'' A young man who was a slightly paler copy of Michael strode into the lobby, and Heather immediately flew to him.

"Come on, Dave, I want you to meet Susan; Susan, my little brother, David.''

The scene had played before her eyes like a movie on a screen. Susan held out her hand to Michael's brother, feeling so weak in the knees she almost curtsied.

"I wanted to tell him, Heather,'' David said.

"I know, darling, but we just met in the lobby, and you couldn't expect me to keep it a secret!''

"Hardly! Let's announce it to the convention!'' And with a jaunty wave David bore his beloved off.

"Heather's going to be your sister-in-law?'' Susan still couldn't believe it.

"Isn't it great! They've been head-over-heels for each other for ages. It's about time they made it official.''

Susan's circulation was beginning to work again and she felt herself returning to normal. "Is David a lawyer already?'' Her voice still sounded weak to her own ears.

"Won't take the bar exam until this fall, but he just finished his law school exams so he came over for the convention and to interview.''

"Interview?''

Michael nodded, pulling Susan's hand through his own and walking across the lobby toward the beach. "He wants to clerk in the islands, at least for the summer. Of course, I hope he'll eventually go into practice with me, but he'll take both the Washington and Hawaii bars so he'll be licensed in both states.''

Susan nodded. Michael grinned at her and placed a

tiny peck of a kiss behind her ear. "Enough of my family history," he said. "Let's go on a picnic!"

"So Heather will be looking for a job here?" Susan mused as they reached the sand. "I just might know of an opening."

Susan was delighted when she discovered that Michael's plan for the picnic called for sailing to the beach in a small catamaran. And not just any beach; they were going back to Bali Ha'i. As the sun sparkled on the water and a pleasant breeze puffed out the white jib, Susan struggled inwardly with her conflicting desires. She wanted to enjoy the day; she wanted to enjoy being alone with Michael. But she wanted to protect herself against the hurt that she knew had to lie at the end of it all. If only their story could have the happy ending that Lani and Kele's and Heather and David's did.

She unfastened the buttons holding her slit skirt together and let it fall open to reveal the shorts underneath. Then she kicked off her sandals and rubbed suntan oil on her arms and legs before leaning back on the cushions lining her seat. Michael expertly set the mainsail, and Susan watched lazily as he guided the rudder to take them northward around the island. Seagulls glided and swooped overhead against the blue sky; the waves gently rocked the little craft, lulling her as she breathed deeply of the fresh salt air.

After a time Michael locked the wheel on course and came to sit by her. "Where did you learn to sail?" Susan asked. It seemed he never failed to surprise her with his many talents.

"When I was a kid, David and I used to take them out all the time."

"When you weren't burying pirate treasure behind the waterfall?"

"That's right." He picked up her ringless left hand and ran his fingers over it gently. "It sure looks better this way. Do you want to tell me about it?"

172

Susan knew she owed him some kind of explanation. But what could she say? *I'm so madly in love with you that I'd try anything to forget you? I was hurt when you didn't write, and I could see you didn't care for me as much as I did for you, so I took Josh on the rebound?*

"Josh was an old boyfriend. He came to see me. I thought it would work. Then I realized it wouldn't."

He raised her hand to his lips and kissed each finger, then turned it over and kissed the palm. "That's good enough for me," he said.

The Kilauea lighthouse came into view on their left—or port, as Michael informed her it should be called—and he got up to change their course. "Want a sailing lesson?" he asked.

Susan jumped up to join him. She put her hands on the wheel as he directed her, then he stood behind, his hands over hers, and guided her as she steered the boat around the point. When they were sailing due east, Michael locked the rudder again into position so they could sit down. But he didn't get far away from the wheel because, he explained, the water was sometimes rougher on that side of the island.

They sat quietly for several minutes, listening to the gentle slapping sounds of the sea against the hulls of the cat, the breeze ruffling the sails, and the calls of the sea birds around them. Then Susan remembered something she needed to say. "Michael, thank you for the orchids. They were lovely."

He gave her a slow, broad smile in reply. "I didn't want you to think I had forgotten you. I had been working literally night and day since the plane touched down in Seattle. It always seemed that the only time I could find myself free even to call you would be something like four A.M. here and I didn't think you'd care too much for that."

"But you managed to get away early?" She hadn't

meant for the question to sound loaded, but that was the way it came out.

"That was one of the reasons I was working around the clock—so I could get back here. I'm afraid a lawyer's life is often like that. It would be pretty hard for a wife to put up with."

Susan gasped at the implication of the comment, but before she could reply, the boat ran into a spot of rough water and Michael was required at the helm. He stayed at the wheel to steer them around the point and into Hanalei Bay. If Lumahai Beach was breathtaking approached by car, it was unbelievable by boat. The sweep of the white crescent beach, washed by rolling white-fringed blue waves, shone like silver in the sun. And ahead of them, rising from its base of dark green foliage like a queen above kneeling suppliants, was the majestic Bali Ha'i, calling to them to come to her.

The little catamaran washed smoothly onto the beach, riding the crest of a snowy wave and then coming to rest with scratching and scraping sounds on the sandy beach. Michael jumped ashore, pulled the boat farther up for a more secure mooring, and then helped Susan jump down.

"Are you hungry?" he asked.

"Not yet," she replied. She wanted to feast on the beauty around her first—and on what he had said.

"Good, let's walk a little, then," he suggested and held out his hand.

Hand-in-hand they strolled leisurely along the edge of the water, the waves washing over their feet.

"It's paradise," Susan said exuberantly with a swing of her arm to include the sand, sea, sky, and mountain. "How could there be so much intense beauty in one spot?"

As the words left her mouth she regretted them and tensed for a pious, "God-created-it", answer. But instead Michael drew her closer to him and mur-

174

mured, "That's what I wonder every time I look at you."

She responded to the deep thrill of tenderness in his voice and to the urgent pressure of his kiss as he drew her into his arms. *If only it could always be like this,* her mind cried. But it couldn't. He knew it, too. He must know. Why was he doing this to her?

Suddenly she pulled away from him and lashed out at the man who a second ago she had been loving so tenderly. Despair over the hopelessness of the situation closed around her, blocking out the sun and the beauty of the day. "Why don't you just leave me alone?" she exclaimed. "You and your God—just leave me alone!"

She tore from him, whirled around, and ran blindly down the beach in the direction they had come. She was almost back to the boat when Michael stopped her, spinning her around to face him with a firm grip on her shoulder.

"All right, I will. But first tell me about it. I think I have a right to know what it's all about."

The energy from her emotional outburst was spent. She dropped on the sand. "Okay, I'll tell you. Then you'll see how totally incompatible our lifestyles are and why we should stop seeing each other. Because I can never believe the way you do."

Michael sat beside her, not touching her, but studying her face closely as she spoke.

"There is a Bible verse, something about 'I will not leave you comfortless or as a lamb in the storm,' " she began. "Well, with a little help from a crooked lawyer He left me." She flung the statement out as a challenge. Her words sounded harsh even to her own ears.

But Michael did not rise to the bait. "Or perhaps you left Him?" he suggested quietly.

"Oh, but not without a long, hard struggle first. I

really tried to live it. Let me give you a few choice examples of my experience of living with Christians. Dear Uncle Charles sent me off to this Holy of Holies Bible college with a suitcase containing exactly three skirts—three cheap skirts because neither of us could scrape together enough money for decent ones. So they shrank. But college rules decreed skirts must touch the floor when the wearer was kneeling.

"One of the more exemplary Christian girls on campus turned me in to the dean of women—who by the way was married but her husband lived elsewhere. Anyway, I was called before the discipline committee, which met every Wednesday night after prayer meeting. I was commanded to kneel. My skirt didn't touch the floor. I was given demerits."

Just the faintest flicker of a smile crossed Michael's face. "I'll bet you looked good in those skirts."

"It might sound funny to you," she flared, "but if you got too many demerits you were sent home. I didn't have a home to be sent to. And then I got demerits when my grades dropped. Lights went out at ten o'clock. All the other kids studied with flashlights under their covers, but I wouldn't cheat. You see, I was really trying. But then my grades fell because I was competing with kids who cheated on study hours.

"Next I got in trouble for working too many hours. Uncle Charles paid my tuition, but that was all—I had to provide the rest. So I got three housecleaning jobs, a babysitting job, a job making ice cream at a drive-in, and a job as a file clerk for a class ring company. They were all part-time on call, but everything would come up at once—like during finals week. Sometimes I worked up to forty hours a week, and we were allowed only twenty a week by college rules. So of course I got called in again. They actually told me they realized I needed the money, but they were 'morally obligated to scold me.' And when I had to work on Sundays I was charged with not having enough faith.

"Then there was the President's wife who was an ex-hurdle jumper. She wore brown, gray, and navy blue exclusively, and had Authority down to a fine science. She would lecture us about the 'temptations of being a young woman' and recount dramatically for us how she would 'pray to God that he would help me save myself for the right man.' And I always thought, *Nothing to worry about, lady*."

At that Michael's vow of silence was shattered with a chuckle. Susan smiled in return, then went on.

"And there was Moira, the physical ed teacher who was the self-appointed policeman of the six-inch rule. Men and women couldn't touch each other—not even when we were having a fight. But we could spend one hour a week sitting in the dating parlor—which we called the fishbowl because it had floor-to-ceiling windows. So Moira spent her evenings walking around the outside of the parlor and reporting students who tried anything sinful like holding hands."

This vignette was greeted with more than a chuckle. Michael shook his head and laughed, "I can just picture it! Is there more?"

"Oh, yes, indeed," and now Susan smiled broadly, too. "There was the rule against members of the opposite sex in practice rooms in the music building. I liked to play jazz with a fellow from Texas, so I would stand in the doorway while he would play something, then I would try to play it while he stood in the doorway and watched. One day I got too excited about the music and we wound up in the same room."

"More demerits?"

"You guessed it," Susan laughed. "Oh yes, and I also got demerits for going to church too early—with a boy, of course—and for leaving my toothbrush out."

"Leaving your toothbrush out?" Michael was laughing helplessly by now.

"Yes, of course. Christians are tidy. But we did get a bit of our own back on the six-inch rule. That winter we had an ice storm. If a female student fell on the ice and a gentleman helped her up, they both got demerits. One glorious day the dean of women fell on the ice and no fewer than seven male students stood around shaking their heads and saying how sorry they were."

By the end of the story they were both convulsed with laughter. Finally they had to stop and wipe their eyes and catch their breath. Michael was the first to recover his voice. "You've learned a very important lesson, haven't you? You can't earn your salvation. That's why God offers it as a free gift—because our efforts are so silly."

He became suddenly serious. "Those poor people. Working so desperately to earn something that needs only to be accepted on faith. I feel awfully sorry for them, don't you?"

Susan quit laughing now, too. "Yes, I do." She said it slowly, then burst into smiles. "Yes, I really do! I feel terribly sorry for them all! All that time I hated them, and they were really just so funny and so pitiful. Oh, Michael, you don't know what it's done for me to see that!"

"I hope you see, too, that practicing what *they* were preaching had nothing to do with real Christianity—nothing to do with a personal relationship with Jesus Christ based on love and faith. What they were doing had as much to do with Christianity as the Victorian prudery that demanded a grand piano to be draped so as not to show its legs."

"Yes, I do. I see it all so clearly now," she said, blinking back the tears in her eyes. She didn't even know why the tears were there; she just knew that her heart was full to overflowing.

"Susan," he said, looking down into her eyes, his hands holding hers, "turning your back on manmade rules is one thing. Turning your back on divine love is quite another."

"Yes, I know that now. Oh, Michael, I feel so good, so free, so happy!"

In sharp contrast, the memory of her caustic bitterness and her behavior at the luau engulfed her in humiliation. "I'm so sorry for the way I've acted," she added. "How did you put up with me? Can you ever forgive me?" She hung her head.

"Of course I can. I knew it would be all right somehow. I was praying all the time."

"Oh, yes, you told me once—living by faith." And this time she said it with understanding and acceptance, with no traces of her former acrimony.

His answer was a smile that touched a chord deep within her.

She wanted to jump to her feet and dance on the beach, race with the waves, turn somersaults to express her joy. But Michael had quite a different method of expression in mind. As he took her in his arms and kissed her rapturously, she knew an intense happiness deep within her. Her body thrilled with it. A little sob broke from her, and Susan found herself in a world suffused with a golden glow. Everything about her was bathed in the light of her inner joy—the glory of the moment lighting everything around her with her own luminescence.

"And now," Michael said, caressing her cheek with his finger, "I want to talk about a very human love." He spoke so quietly it was as if the words were kneeling. "My love for you."

And suddenly Susan knew it *was* possible—paradise now and later.

ABOUT THE AUTHOR

DONNA FLETCHER CROW based *Love Unmerited* on a trip she took to Kauai with her Christian lawyer husband. The heroine's lack of a sense of direction is autobiographical. But in spite of time lost from turning the wrong way out of elevators and walking in wet cememt, Donna is the mother of four children and the author of cookbooks, children's books, contemporary romances, and historical novels.

A Letter to Our Readers

Dear Reader:

Welcome to the world of Serenade Books—a series designed to bring you the most beautiful love stories in the world of inspirational romance. They will uplift you, encourage you, and provide hours of wholesome entertainment, so thousands of readers have testified. In order that we might better contribute to your reading enjoyment, we would appreciate your taking a few minutes to respond to the following questions and return to:

> Editor, Serenade Books
> The Zondervan Publishing House
> 1415 Lake Drive, S.E.
> Grand Rapids, Michigan 49506

1. Did you enjoy reading LOVE UNMERITED?

   ☐ Very much. I would like to see more books by this author!
   ☐ Moderately
   ☐ I would have enjoyed it more if _____

   _____

2. Where did you purchase this book? _____

3. What influenced your decision to purchase this book?

   ☐ Cover   ☐ Back cover copy
   ☐ Title   ☐ Friends
   ☐ Publicity   ☐ Other _____

4. What are some inspirational themes you would like to see treated in future books?

_____

5. Please indicate your age range:
   ☐ Under 18   ☐ 25–34   ☐ 46–55
   ☐ 18–24   ☐ 35–45   ☐ Over 55

6. If you are interested in receiving information about our Serenade Home Reader Service, in which you will be offered new and exciting novels on a regular basis, please give us your name and address. (This does NOT obligate you for membership.)

Name _____

Occupation _____

Address _____

City _____ State _____ Zip _____

Serenade / Saga books are inspirational romances in historical settings, designed to bring you a joyful, heart-lifting reading experience.

Serenade / Saga books available in your local book store:

Serenade / Serenata books are inspirational romances in contemporary settings, designed to bring you a joyful, heart-lifting reading experience.

Serenade / Serenata books available in your local bookstore:

#1 *On Wings of Love*, Elaine L. Schulte
#2 *Love's Sweet Promise*, Susan C. Feldhake
#3 *For Love Alone*, Susan C. Feldhake
#4 *Love's Late Spring*, Lydia Heermann
#5 *In Comes Love*, Mab Graff Hoover
#6 *Fountain of Love*, Velma S. Daniels and Peggy E. King.
#7 *Morning Song*, Linda Herring
#8 *A Mountain to Stand Strong*, Peggy Darty
#9 *Love's Perfect Image*, Judy Baer
#10 *Smoky Mountain Sunrise*, Yvonne Lehman
#11 *Greengold Autumn*, Donna Fletcher Crow
#12 *Irresistible Love*, Elaine Anne McAvoy
#13 *Eternal Flame*, Lurlene McDaniel
#14 *Windsong*, Linda Herring
#15 *Forever Eden*, Barbara Bennett
#16 *Call of the Dove*, Madge Harrah
#17 *The Desires of Your Heart*, Donna Fletcher Crow
#18 *Tender Adversary*, Judy Baer
#19 *Halfway to Heaven*, Nancy Johanson
#20 *Hold Fast the Dream*, Lurlene McDaniel
#21 *The Disguise of Love*, Mary LaPietra
#22 *Through a Glass Darkly*, Sara Mitchell
#23 *More Than a Summer's Love*, Yvonne Lehman
#24 *Language of the Heart*, Jeanne Anders
#25 *One More River*, Suzanne Pierson Ellison
#26 *Journey Toward Tomorrow*, Karyn Carr
#27 *Flower of the Sea*, Amanda Clark

Watch for other books in both the *Serenade/Saga* (historical) and *Serenade/Serenata* (contemporary) series coming soon.